The Forgotten Adventures of

SHERLOCK
HOLMES

H. PAUL JEFFERS

The Forgotten Adventures of

SHERLOCK HOLMES

**Based on the Original Radio Plays
by Anthony Boucher and Denis Green**

CARROLL & GRAF PUBLISHERS
NEW YORK

THE FORGOTTEN ADVENTURES OF SHERLOCK HOLMES

Carroll & Graf Publishers
An Imprint of Avalon Publishing Group Inc.
245 West 17th Street
11th Floor
New York, NY 10011

AVALON
publishing group incorporated

First Carroll & Graf edition 2005

Library of Congress Cataloging-in-Publication Data is available.

ISBN: 0-7867-1587-1

Printed in the United States of America
Interior design by Jamie McNeely
Distributed by Publishers Group West

For Mike "Wiggins" Whelan,
Commissionaire of the Baker Street Irregulars,
with gratitude for "the shilling."

· CONTENTS ·

· ACKNOWLEDGMENTS ·

The Sherlock Holmes short stories in this book are based on the following radio dramas in the series "The New Adventures of Sherlock Holmes" by Anthony Boucher and Denis Green:

"In Flanders Fields" (Broadcast May 14, 1945)

"The Paradol Chamber" (Broadcast May 21, 1945)

"The Accidental Murderess" (Broadcast November 26, 1945)

"The Adventure of the Blarney Stone" (Broadcast March 18, 1946)

"The Book of Tobit" (Broadcast March 26, 1945)

"The Haunting of Sherlock Holmes" (Broadcast May 20, 1946)

"The Adventure of the Stuttering Ghost" (Broadcast October 12, 1946)

"The Clue of the Hungry Cat" (Broadcast October 26, 1946)

"The Singular Affair of the Dying Schoolboys" (Broadcast November 9, 1946)

"The Adventure of the *Sally Martin*" (Broadcast November 23, 1946)

"The Adventure of the Grand Old Man" (Broadcast December 21, 1946)

"The Darlington Substitution" (Broadcast January 4, 1947)

"The Adventure of Maltree Abbey" (Broadcast March 31, 1947)

· FOREWORD ·

Mystery in the Air

I play the game for the game's own sake.

—Sherlock Holmes, *The Adventure of the
Bruce-Partington Plans*

*D*uring the darkest years of the Great Depression and throughout World War Two, millions of Americans who switched on radios in their parlors, kitchens, and bedrooms seeking respite in the evening from their personal problems and worries about the world found it once a week by spending half an hour in the company of one of the world's most engaging storytellers while Dr. John H. Watson recalled tales of adventures with Sherlock Holmes of 221B Baker

Street, London. Created by Arthur Conan Doyle in four novels and fifty-six short stories, from 1887 to 1927, known to Sherlockians as "the Sacred Writings" and "the Canon," the fictional detective was not only literature's most enduring and beloved crime solver, but the movies' most frequently portrayed character. "The whole Sherlock Holmes saga," wrote author and essayist Christopher Morley in the preface to the first single-volume compendium of the Canon (*The Complete Sherlock Holmes*, published in 1938), "is a triumphant illustration of art's supremacy over life."

Morley had been one of the founders of a group of Holmes enthusiasts and 1930s literary lights called "The Baker Street Irregulars." The name was adopted from that of a motley band of London street urchins whom Holmes occasionally engaged at the wages of a shilling each to assist in his investigations, because they could "go everywhere, see everything, overhear anyone" unnoticed. The premise of the BSI was (and is) playing an intellectual game in which Holmes and Watson are real and Arthur Conan Doyle was merely Watson's literary agent.

This mind sport was explained by Vincent Starrett in *The Private Life of Sherlock Holmes*. "Let us speak, and speak again, of Sherlock Holmes," he wrote. "For the plain fact is, gentlemen, that the imperishable detective is still a more commanding figure in the world than most of the warriors and statesmen in whose present existence we are invited to believe."

Born in the year that the Baker Street Irregulars was founded, I first met Holmes over the radio. Because my favorite shows were the mystery and detective programs, among them *The Shadow* and *Mr. District Attorney,* I was introduced to the Sleuth of Baker Street in 1941 at the age of seven in a weekly broadcast called "The New Adventures of Sherlock

Holmes." I already knew the stars of the show, Basil Rathbone as Holmes and Nigel Bruce as Watson, from seeing them in Sherlock Holmes movies at the Rialto theater in Phoenixville, Pennsylvania. The first were *The Adventures of Sherlock Holmes* and *The Hound of the Baskervilles*. In the next few years, I watched twelve more, set in modern times, from *The Voice of Terror* to *Dressed to Kill*.

My introduction to Sherlock on the pages of a book was the result of my searching the fiction shelves of the public library at about age ten. Seeking something exciting, I found a fat volume containing all the Conan Doyle stories and novels and read them all, from the novel *A Study in Scarlet* to the last thrilling short story, "The Adventure of the Retired Colourman," for a total of 1323 pages.

While I cannot claim to have listened to all of the Holmes radio shows in the years in which the program was on the air throughout the 1940s, I missed very few. I'd started tuning in when I was seven years old. When the series went off the air, I was a sophomore in high school.

While planning a career in journalism and hoping to one day become a published author, I learned of the Baker Street Irregulars and yearned to join it. But I hadn't a clue as to what might be required to qualify for membership or even where it was located, except that it held an annual dinner in New York City. Because I'd always wanted to take a try at writing a mystery novel, and feeling confident in my accrued knowledge of Sherlock Holmes, I decided to attempt one with him as the main character. I teamed a very young Sherlock with one of my true American heroes, Theodore Roosevelt, in *The Adventure of the Stalwart Companions*. Set in New York in the summer of 1880, a year before Holmes met Watson, when Sherlock was in the United States as an actor with a touring Shakespearian troupe and Teddy Roosevelt was fresh out of Harvard, the novel involved a political murder. The story was related in a long-lost manuscript by Roosevelt I'd "discovered." To my amazement, it was published in 1978 by Harper & Row.

Even more astonishingly, the book brought me an invitation to attend the next dinner of the BSI. This resulted in *Murder Most Irregular* (1983), in which someone is killing members of the BSI, using methods found in the Holmesian Canon. After several years, I was granted BSI membership in the form of an "investiture" in the name of Wilson Hargreave, a detective with the New York Police Bureau who had been named but not seen in the Canon. I'd used him as the policeman who alerted Sherlock and Teddy to the murder that had been committed in Gramercy Park in *Stalwart Companions*.

I find myself undertaking adaptations of thirteen of the Holmes radio programs I'd listened to while growing up in Pennsylvania, not because I was regarded as an authority about Sherlock, but as the consequence of the happy coincidence that my literary agent also represents a group of Sherlockians who had discovered recordings of radio's "New Adventures of Sherlock Holmes." They had made them available on audio cassettes and later in a book of thirteen short stories, adapted by Ken Greenwald, titled *The Lost Adventures of Sherlock Holmes* (1993).

In this second collection of adventures written by a remarkable pair of radio writers, Anthony Boucher and Denis Green and broadcast from June 1945 to March 1947, the game is again afoot with Holmes and Watson as they tackle mysteries that range from a blood-soaked World War One battlefield to strange doings at Maltree Abbey. They also confront the puzzle of the accidental murderess, the haunting of Sherlock Holmes, and the adventure of the stuttering ghost. They ponder the clue of the hungry cat, some dying schoolboys, the Book of Tobit, the Paradol Chamber, the ship *Sally Martin,* the Darlington Substitution, and the case of the Grand Old Man.

Radio was theater of the mind. The listener heard the voices of the actors, sound effects, and mood music and transformed them by imagination into scenes as vivid and compelling as if the listener were watching the drama unfolding on a stage or screen. "The listener produced half the show right in his own head," wrote social commentator Brock Brower in "A Lament for Old-time Radio" in *Esquire* magazine in April 1960, "taking his lead from a range of voices, a musical bridge, and a few sound effects."

While the vast audiences for "The New Adventures of Sherlock Holmes" had no trouble envisioning him and Dr. Watson in action in whatever situations Boucher and Green devised, translating radio programs to be *read* as short stories necessitates occasional expansion of the original texts to take the place of the radio listener's imagination, giving additional information, inserting narrative for a sound effect or musical element, and providing context. In doing so, I have tried to remain true to Boucher and Green and, of course, to Sir Arthur Conan Doyle / Dr. Watson, while preserving the unique character of the programs that made "The New Adventures of Sherlock Holmes" the longest-running mystery drama in the Golden Age of Radio.

I hope that in reading these stories you will discover, as did I and millions of Americans who heard them on the air so long ago, that Christopher Morley was right when he wrote that "no fiction character ever created has become so charmingly real."

H. Paul Jeffers,
"Wilson Hargreave," Baker Street Irregular

· INTRODUCTION ·

A Singular Partnership

*I*n retrospect, it seems inevitable that as radio became the primary (and cheapest) means of entertainment for Americans in the depths of history's worst and longest economic crisis Sherlock Holmes and his faithful friend and biographer Dr. John H. Watson would attract listeners. Yet, when a young actress and vaudevillian, Edith Meiser, who had been a devoted fan of Sir Arthur Conan Doyle since the age of ten, wrote adaptations of two Holmes short stories as radio dramas and took the scripts to the National Broadcasting Company (NBC) program department, she was told that while the material was "good," the likelihood of finding an advertiser to sponsor an unproved format was unpromising.

What advertisers on radio shows wanted in 1930, she was

informed, were comedy and musical fare. Undaunted, Meiser
began pitching the idea directly to advertising agencies. The
sponsor that took the chance on bringing Mr. Holmes and Dr.
Watson into America's homes was George Washington Coffee.
The result was a broadcast on October 30, 1930, of an adapta-
tion of "The Speckled Band." Holmes was played by the world's
most famous Holmes impersonator, William Gillette (the first
actor to play him on the stage, he had made a lifetime career of
it). Dr. Watson was enacted by Leigh Lovel.

Because Gillette felt uncomfortable with the radio medium,
he was replaced by Clive Brook for two shows. Richard Gordon
finally settled into the role from November 1930 to May
1933. He was succeeded on November 11, 1934, by Louis
Hector, but for only one season. His final episode was May 26,
1935. (It was also Leigh Lovell's last show. He died in August.)

On February 1, 1936, Richard Gordon returned to the
role of Holmes, with Harry West as Watson. The sponsor was
the Household Finance Corporation. The network was now the
Mutual Broadcasting System. Gordon and West continued in
their roles until the end of this series on December 24, 1936.
Louis Hector again played Holmes, but on an NBC television
broadcast on November 27, 1937. It was Holmes's first
appearance on the small screen.

The following year, Holmes was brought to radio by the Mercury Theater of the Air, with its founder-director-star, Orson
Welles, as "The Immortal Sherlock Holmes." Holmes went on
the air a month before Welles scared the country out of its wits
with a far-too-realistic radio production of "War of the Worlds"
that convinced millions of people that the United States was
under attack by men from Mars in horrible machines emitting
a death ray.

The definitive Homes on radio made his debut the following year. Basil Rathbone and Nigel Bruce, who had created Holmes and Watson on the screen in two successful films and who would make 12 more during the course of their radio portrayals, brought them to vivid life in "The New Adventures of Sherlock Holmes" in October of that year. Edith Meiser continued to adapt Conan Doyle stories and write new ones, with the help of famed mystery novelist and the creator of "The Saint," Leslie Charteris (using the pseudonym Bruce Taylor). Other writers were Denis Green, Max Ehrlich, Howard Merrill, Leonard Lee, and Anthony Boucher.

Denis Green had been a writer for *The Adventures of the Thin Man*. A weekly radio show based on the Dashiell Hammett novel, the program made its debut in 1941. Born in England, Green had been a stage actor and production manager for his old friend Leslie Howard, who later portrayed Ashley Wilkes in *Gone With the Wind*. When Howard came to the United Sates, he invited Green to accompany him. As part of the so-called British Colony in Hollywood before and during World War Two, Green had small roles in several feature films, including the first two Basil Rathbone-Nigel Bruce films in 1939, *The Adventures of Sherlock Holmes* and *The Hound of the Baskervilles,* followed by *Waterloo Bridge* (1940) and *Dr. Jekyll and Mr. Hyde, A Yank in the R.A.F., Scotland Yard,* and *They Met in Bombay,* all in 1941.

Hired by Leslie Charteris as the head writer for the Sherlock Holmes radio productions, Green in turn engaged Boucher when Charteris left the show. As radio historian John Dunning noted in *On the Air: The Encyclopedia of Old-Time Radio* (1998), the Boucher-Green teaming was "a long-distance partnership," with Boucher living in San Francisco and Green residing in Los Angeles. Boucher came up with the plots. Green's job was to devise the dialogue. Like the Holmes and Watson pairing, they formed a singular partnership.

Half-hour programs broadcast from Hollywood, the Holmes shows were heard on various nights at different times on NBC, Blue Network (NBC), Mutual Broadcasting System, and ABC, from Sundays at 7:00 P.M. to Fridays at 8:30 P.M. Each began with a retired Dr. Watson greeting a visitor (the show's announcer) and inviting him to "draw up a chair by the fire" while Watson reminisced about a Sherlock Holmes case with pauses in the show to sell George Washington Coffee and subsequently Petri Wine and Bromo Quinine. Later sponsors were Kreml Hair Tonic and Trimount Clipper Craft. The chatty sales pitches were integrated into the program as Dr. Watson paused in the tale at a cliff-hanger moment. The yarns were augmented by scene-evoking music and sound effects. In a review of the series, a critic for a radio magazine wrote, "You can almost see the swirling and eerie fog of Baker Street."

While Holmes had ventured into American living rooms by way of radio in 1930, he was late in doing so in his own country. The British Broadcasting Corporation (BBC) did not bring him to the air waves in the United Kingdom until 1943. Sherlock was Arthur Wontner, who had played him in several early films. The BBC's longest running series featured Norman Shelley and Carleton Hobbs, (1952–1969), but England's most memorable radio Holmes was one of Britain's most distinguished actors, John Gielgud, with Ralph Richardson as the good doctor, in a popular series during the mid-1950s.

Between 1930 and the end of the 1950s the total number of broadcasts in the United States and Britain was 643. Of these, Edith Meiser wrote or co-wrote 260 (1939–1945).

Those by Anthony Boucher, Denis Green, and Bruce Taylor (Charteris) totaled 117 (1945–1947). In their first year with Rathbone as Holmes, the team produced 39 scripts, of which four were taken from Sir Arthur Conan Doyle's stories. With the departure of Rathbone in 1946, the Sleuth of Baker Street was succeeded by a series of actors, beginning with Tom Conway (a movie actor who played "The Falcon" and Bulldog Drummond and was the brother of the A-list movie star George Sanders). Nigel Bruce stayed on as the good doctor. By the fall of 1950, he and Conway were gone, replaced by John Stanley and Alfred Shirley, and then by Ben Wright and Eric Snowden. By this time, television was rapidly displacing radio as the main source of home entertainment, including the first TV Holmes. With Sherlock played by Ronald Howard (son of Leslie Howard), the series was produced on the cheap in Europe.

Although Boucher and Green continued writing for "The New Adventures of Sherlock Holmes" after Rathbone's departure, with him gone and the ultimate departure of Nigel Bruce, the program lost its magic and soon went off the air. This did not mean the end of the Boucher-Green partnership. Asked by Petri Wines to create a show "just like Sherlock Holmes," they came up with "The Casebook of Gregory Hood." The title character lived in San Francisco and was an antiques dealer and amateur detective. The program took over the Holmes time slot and remained on the air on Mutual through 1949. In sponsoring the show, Petri Wines no longer had to pay $1,000 a week to the Arthur Conan Doyle estate for the right to use Holmes, and the writers were not bound to set their stories long ago in England. Although Rathbone had abandoned Holmes, he did not give up playing a London detective. He became

"Scotland Yard's Inspector Burke" on a show that ran for less than a year (January 21–December 29,1947).

Like the character brought to life in radio scripts for three seasons, Anthony Boucher was a man with broad interests and an inquisitive nature that ranged from science and great music to languages, creating and solving puzzles and exploring criminality, both true and fictional. Born in Oakland, California, on August 21, 1911, William Anthony Parker White ignored the advice of Sherlock Holmes that it is always "awkward doing business with an alias" and earned vaunted reputations for his brilliant writing in the fields of science fiction, mystery stories, and literary and music criticism, and as an editor. Using the names Anthony Boucher and H. H. H. Holmes, he reviewed detective stories for *Ellery Queen's Mystery Magazine* and the *New York Times Book Review;* fantasy and science fiction for the *New York Times,* Chicago *Sun-Times,* and the *New York Herald Tribune;* and musical performances for the *Opera News.* Between 1949 and 1958, he was editor of the *Magazine of Fantasy and Science Fiction.* As Anthony Boucher, he also edited *True Crime Detective* magazine (1952–1953), half a dozen detection anthologies, the Mercury Mysteries (1952–1955), the Dell Great Mystery Library (1957–1960), and the Collier Mystery Classics (1962–1968).

Among Boucher's fictional works were numerous short stories and detective novels, including *The Case of the Seven of Calvary* (1937), *The Case of the Crumpled Knave* (1939), *Nine Times Nine* (1940), *The Case of the Baker Street Irregulars* (1940, reprinted as *Blood on Baker Street*), *The Case of the Solid Key* (1941), *Rocket to the Morgue* (1942), and *The Case of the Seven Sneezes* (1942). Three collections of short stories are *Far and Away; Eleven Fantasy and SF Stories* (1955), *The Compleat Werewolf and Other Stories of Fantasy and SF* (1969), and

Exeunt Murderers (The Best Mystery Stories of Anthony Boucher) edited by Francis M. Nevins, Jr., and Martin H. Greenberg (1983). Writing as H. H. H. Holmes, he provided *Nine Times Nine* and *Rocket to the Morgue,* featuring the detective Sister Ursula, a nun of the fictional Order of St. Martha of Bethany.

In *The Case of the Baker Street Irregulars,* a devoted member of the Sherlockian society finds himself entangled in a Hollywood murder case with clues taken from the Sir Arthur Conan Doyle stories, They include a dancing-men cipher, five orange pips, *Rache* scrawled in blood on walls, a gun whisked away on a string as in "The Problem of Thor Bridge," an aluminum crutch, the dog that did not bark in the night-time, a severed ear in a cardboard box, a Sussex vampire and "Ricoletti" of the clubfoot and his "abominable wife."

Recipient of the Mystery Writers of America's Edgar Allan Poe award for excellence in criticism in 1946, 1950 and 1953, he served as MWA president in 1951. Two years after he died of lung cancer in 1968, American detective fans began holding annual conclaves in his memory. Officially called the Anthony Boucher Memorial Mystery Convention, they're popularly known as "Bouchercons." Denis Green continued to write, but eventually returned to acting, appearing on such TV shows as *Rawhide* and *Wagon Train*. He died in the 1960s.

On learning of Boucher's death, Frederick Dannay, cocreator of "Ellery Queen," said, "In his chosen field Tony was a Renaissance man, a complete man—writer, critic and historian."

"Good detective stories are," Boucher wrote, "ever valuable in retrospect as indirect but vivid pictures of the society from which they spring." In writing scripts for radio's "The New Adventures of Sherlock Holmes," thirteen of which are the basis for the stories in this book, he undertook with great success the challenge of carrying the program's audiences back to a time recalled by a contemporary, Vincent Starrett. He asked, "Shall they not always live in Baker Street? Are they not there this moment as one writes? Outside, the hansoms rattle through the rain . . . Within, the sea coal flames upon the hearth and Holmes and Watson take their well-won ease. So they will live for all that love them well, in a romantic chamber of the heart, in a nostalgic country of the mind, where it is always 1895."

· 1 ·

In Flanders Fields

*B*efore relating the singular affair that until now has been one of the most guarded secrets of the Great War in the files of His Majesty's War Office, I must begin by recalling that in the early months of 1914, Sherlock Holmes had come out of retirement to proffer his remarkable combination of intellectual acumen, practical activity, a gift for masquerade, and talents as an actor at the disposal of the government, with historical results. In the guise and with the accent of an Irish-American by the name of Altamont, my friend thwarted the dastardly schemes of the German agent Von Bork to obtain the plans of England's military preparedness and devices of national defense. With the scoundrel trussed up in an automobile outside Von Bork's headquarters on the

Channel coast, and his network of spies and traitors nullified, Holmes placed a hand upon my shoulder and said, "Stand with me here upon the terrace, my friend, for it may be the last quiet talk that we shall have."

"Surely not, Holmes," I objected in a tone of alarm as I turned to him. "We both have many years ahead of us."

Chatting serenely for the next few minutes, we recalled adventures of our shared past, going back more than two decades, in which England and its premier city had been made better and safer because of the presence and unfailing vigilance of the best and wisest man I had ever known. Presently, he looked out at the moonlit sea, shook a thoughtful head, and said quietly, "There is an east wind coming, Watson."

"I think not, Holmes," I replied "It is very warm."

"Good old, Watson," said he, with an affectionate smile. "You are the one fixed point in a changing age. There's an east wind coming all the same, such a wind as never blew on England yet. It will be cold and bitter, Watson, and a good many of us may wither before its blast. But it's God's own wind none the less, and a cleaner, better, stronger land will lie in the sunshine when the storm has cleared."

The next time I saw Holmes was in the autumn of the first year of the Great War that he had forecast as we stood that day upon the terrace. With the Von Bork affair completed, he had returned to his studies of philosophy and agriculture on a small farm upon the Sussex downs five miles from Eastbourne. Living a hermitlike life of keeping bees, he again vowed his retirement was a permanent one and refused the most princely offers to take up various cases. Therefore, it was with an expression of astonishment that I found him standing in the consulting room of my medical practice in Harley Street on that September morning and exclaiming, "You must leave aside everything, my friend. For crown and country, we are needed in Paris at once."

The case proved to be that of a general's aide de camp who had gone missing and was believed to have either betrayed his country or been kidnapped by German agents. He had in fact, Holmes quickly deduced, simply fallen in love with a saucy dancer from the cancan line of the Moulin Rouge and run off with her for a tryst on the Riviera.

With the matter resolved, I was anxious to return to England and resume my practice and voluntary work in war hospitals. Things were not going well for the Allies at the time. The Germans were advancing on Paris, and the picture was looking very black. It was twenty-four hours before the Battle of the Marne, an engagement that changed the early course of the war, when Holmes informed me at breakfast in our hotel that we had to go up to the front lines on a mission of the utmost secrecy. "This new summons in a telegram from brother Mycroft in the Foreign Office," he explained, "is in the nature of a command."

And so, on a rainy afternoon, Holmes and I, with the boom of distant cannons in our ears, found ourselves in the front seat of a speeding British army staff car. The rear was occupied by two civilians, a handsome woman, and a distinguished-looking man, several years her senior. In one of those moments to which I had become accustomed to believing that Holmes was able to read my thoughts, Holmes leaned toward me and whispered, "He is a Shakespearean actor of some note, though he never achieved the fame to which he thinks he's entitled. I should not be at all surprised if he feels that he's been slighted in not receiving a knighthood."

"How can you possibly deduce all that from just looking at the man?"

"Elementary, my dear fellow," said Holmes as he gazed out at the war-torn landscape. "I didn't deduce it. We saw him twice last year in the London Theater, if you remember. His name is Maitland Morris. He and his wife Cynthia are renowned for their interpretations of *Macbeth*. I haven't seen them in it, but Mycroft attests that her Lady Macbeth is the finest he's ever seen."

"What do you suppose they are doing up here at the front lines?"

"According to Mycroft, his brother is General Sir Stanley Morris, who is in command of this sector of the front. It would seem reasonable to presume that he and Mrs. Morris have come up here to give a performance for the front line troops."

"Quite laudable of them. Very patriotic!"

With the vehicle sloshing and jolting its way toward the battlefield, the driver inquired, "Am I driving too fast for you?"

"No, Sergeant, not at all," said Holmes, sounding as excited as the Holmes of the past.

"No, no, you're doing a splendid job, Driver," I said, "considering the state of the road."

With the sounds of guns growing louder and nearer, Holmes peered ahead, his gray eyes alight and scanning the horizon as he said, "I imagine we've not much farther to go, Sergeant."

"No, sir. We're nearly there."

Although I had seen war firsthand while serving in the army in the Second Afghan War and I had followed the course of this war and read accounts of the devastation it had wreaked on the French countryside as reported in newspapers, I was unprepared for the ghastly reality that unfolded before my eyes from the front seat of the automobile. I found a wasteland of deep holes gouged by artillery shells, blasted and denuded trees, and shattered structures. The grim vista was made even more bleak by a low ceiling of slate-gray clouds and incessant, cold rain.

Presently, when the car slowed and came to a halt, the shelling we'd heard had stopped.

"This is as far as we can go in an automobile," said the driver. "We're four miles from the front. If a German reconnaissance airplane were to spot us, we'd be an easy target. General Morris's headquarters are in a farmhouse beyond that clump of trees. There is a sentry post on the way where you'll be asked to state the password and to produce your papers. I trust they're in order, and that you know the password."

"They are," said Holmes. "I was given the password in Paris. Thank you, Sergeant."

"It's been a pleasure, Mr. Holmes. The best of luck."

Leaving the car, we dashed through the downpour until a burly corporal appeared before us, his rifle upraised. He demanded, "Halt! Who does there?"

"Friend," retorted Holmes.

"Password?"

"Saint Crispin!"

The corporal lowered his rifle. "Approach, friend, and show your papers."

Studying the documents, the soldier shook his head and grinned. "Blimey, this is the last place in the world I'd ever expect to meet Mr. Sherlock Holmes and Dr. John H. Watson. I'll certainly write home to my wife about this. Proceed, gentlemen."

After trudging a few minutes along a narrow, muddy path toward the headquarters, we found ourselves greeted by an impressively tall army officer. Striding boldly toward us with an extended hand, he introduced himself as Captain Maxwell, aide de camp to General Morris. A moment later, we were joined by our companions from the car. Although we had been together for several hours, it was the first time we'd spoken.

"How are you, Mr. Holmes?" said the actor. "I know your brother Mycroft very well. It's a pleasure to meet you, Dr. Watson. I have enjoyed reading your accounts of Mr. Holmes's cases in the *Strand* magazine."

"And I've had the pleasure," said I as we shook hands, "of seeing you and your very charming wife as your leading lady on the stage several times. I presume you are going to give a performance for our gallant troops this evening?"

"Yes, Doctor," said Mrs. Morris. "We're very flattered. They've asked us to do some Shakespeare, although I thought lighter fare would have been more appropriate for men about to go into the front line."

Holmes interjected, "Mr. Morris, I shall look forward to hearing your reading of Henry the Fifth's glorious Saint Crispin speech from the play of that name tonight."

"Bless my soul," exclaimed Morris, "how did you know I was planning to do it?"

"The setting is so perfect and the timing so appropriate," Holmes replied. "I can't think of an English actor who could resist the temptation to speak the greatest appeal to patriotism ever written. One of my fondest memories of my own brief career as an actor with the Sasanoff Company was playing Henry the Fifth in the city of Baltimore in the United States. That was more than thirty years ago, but I remember the speech as vividly as if I'd given it yesterday."

"I had no idea that you once had been an actor, Mr. Holmes," said Mrs. Morris. "What was your most satisfying, which is to say most successful, of all your roles?"

"My performance as Malvolio in *Twelfth Night* garnered some praise from the theatrical critics in New York, but the accolade I prize the most came from Old Baron Dowson the night before he was hanged. He said that in my case what the law had gained the stage had lost."

Drawing a small, leather-bound book from a pocket of his green, rain-slicked macintosh, Maitland Morris declared, "This may seem a little silly to you, Mr. Holmes, but I've been an inveterate autograph collector all my life, and I wonder if you'd mind adding yours to my book."

"Not at all, sir!"

"You'll find yourself among quite distinguished company."

"So I see," said Holmes, leafing through the book. "Angelina Patti. Richard Mansfield, William Gillette. Edwin Booth. The Prince of Wales, now his majesty King George V. The Crown Prince of Norway. And, hello, an inscription by Field Marshal von Taupnitz!"

"Yes, he was one of my admirers when I was in Munich before the war. I suppose now that our countries are fighting, I should tear that page out. You know, I cannot help but feel that art and the appreciation of art are independent of national hatreds."

"Quite so, sir. I carry a medal that was presented to me by the University of Leipzig for some trifling services."

As Holmes returned the signed book to Morris, Captain Maxwell ventured, "We should be moving along. The general is eager to welcome you all."

General Sir Stanley Morris's headquarters was a welcome relief after the dreariness of the war-ravaged landscape and the chilly, soggy trip from Paris. To paraphrase Gilbert and Sullivan, our host appeared to be every bit a modern major general.

With medals and decorations for valor adorning his uniform and a holstered pistol strapped around a trim waist, he was straight as an arrow. As we stepped into a cozy parlor with a cheery fireplace, he said jovially, "It's a long way from Baker Street, Mr. Holmes, but we shall do our best to make you and Dr. Watson feel as much at home as possible."

After greeting his brother and sister-in-law and inviting us to sit by the fire, the general adopted an apologetic tone in describing the arrangements for their performances that evening. "You'll find the stage very primitive," he explained. "It's a platform in a large tent with a curtain made of army blankets. I'm afraid your dressing rooms will be even worse."

"Don't worry about our comfort, Stanley," exclaimed Mrs. Morris. "As long as we cheer the boys up, that's the important thing."

"We're very flattered that they want us to do some Shakespeare," said her husband.

"Rubbish, old boy," retorted the general. "With you and Cynthia up there on the platform, you could read the telephone book, and they'd love you."

"You're very kind. What kind of program have you mapped out for us?"

"I thought we'd have two shows. The tent's not large enough to hold everybody at once. Do you think you can manage two separate shows?"

"Of course I can, Stanley. I may look old, but I don't feel it. May we take a look at the stage and equipment?"

When they were gone in the company of Captain Maxwell, the general leaned forward in his chair with a solemn expression to address Holmes. "I assume," he said gravely, "that I can speak quite freely in front of Dr. Watson."

"With perfect freedom, sir. He's my colleague, and he's an old army man himself."

"Really? What regiment, Doctor?"

"Fifth Northumberland Fusiliers, sir, later attached to the Berkshires in Afghanistan and wounded in the Battle of Maiwand."

"Mr. Holmes, you know why I asked that you come up here so near the front, don't you?"

"You asked for me to be sent here, General?" asked Holmes. Pausing a moment, he said, "Yes, I think I understand."

"Well," I interjected impatiently, "I wish I did."

"You will in good time," Holmes answered.

"In the meanwhile, gentlemen," said the general, "I'll have an orderly show you to your quarters. And Holmes, take a look around, will you, and keep your ears open? We're a very little distance from the front lines, and the German shelling has been going on all day. Now, suddenly, a few hours before we plan to launch a surprise attack, there's this puzzling silence. My concern is that the firing has stopped to allow enemy spies to move through No Man's Land and establish observation posts. Were they to do so, we could lose our advantage. But these are my concerns, not yours, and you've had a long day's journey. I hope you'll find your quarters comfortable. I'll see you at the first of my brother's performances."

Being an old army man, as Holmes had put it, I found our accommodations on the ground floor of a stable that had been converted into officers' quarters much more amenable than some I had known in Afghanistan. While I began unpacking my small valise, Holmes stood pensively at a window, as he had so often done in our sitting room in Baker Street. Oblivious to surroundings and to me, he was lost in contemplation for several minutes.

"You're being very pensive, Holmes," I said.

"Out there in the dark and the rain, only a few miles from here," he said, turning from the window, "are thousands of Germans crouched in trenches and armed and imbued by misguided leaders with a blind, fanatical hatred and the desire to kill and to conquer. Surrounding us are an equal number of English boys, also armed, with a will if not the desire to fight, because they all know their cause is the cause of freedom and justice. All these men are poised to pounce on each other and fight to the death. It's a strange world that we live in, old chap."

For a moment, I felt as though I were twenty years younger, expecting to hear my friend speak of a plan to deal with the latest devilry of his nemesis, Professor Moriarty, the Napoleon of crime, or voice a complaint about the failings of yet another Scotland Yard Inspector. Since leaving General Morris, Holmes had said nothing to enlighten me about why we found ourselves in rude army quarters within cannon range of German artillery. He had often told me that I had the grand gift of silence. Now it was he who exhibited that virtue.

Presently, he declared, "The rain appears to have let up. I believe I'll take the opportunity to have that look around that the general suggested. I won't be gone long."

He returned about half an later and went straight to the window. "Unless I'm mistaken, Watson," he said, "there is something's amiss among the actors."

"Why do you say that?"

"As I was returning from my stroll, I noticed Mrs. Morris in a great state of excitement and hurrying toward the general's headquarters. And now the lady appears to be headed in our direction. And quite upset."

A moment later, the woman burst in. "Mr. Holmes," she cried, "it's Maitland. He's gone missing! Disappeared!"

"Calm yourself," said Holmes. "Tell us what happened."

"We were in our tent making up for the performance, when an orderly came in with a message. Maitland said it was from his brother. He put on his rain coat and said that he would return soon. I waited and waited, and after a while I became worried. I went over to see the general myself. He told me he'd sent no message, and that he hadn't seen any sign of Maitland. What shall I do, Mr. Holmes?"

"You're obviously a patriot, Mrs. Morris. I'm sure that you realize how important it is to the morale of the men that the evening's performance go on as planned."

"Really, Holmes, how can you ask this woman to go on with a show," I objected, "when her husband is missing?"

"There are a thousand men waiting for a moment of diversion," Holmes replied sharply, "many of whom will soon lie dead on the fields of Flanders. They've been promised a show, and it must go on for their sake."

"But how can it go on," asked Mrs. Morris, "without my husband?"

"With your assistance, good lady," Holmes said, "I shall endeavor to take his place."

At times during my long association with Sherlock Holmes, I had marveled at his ability to transform himself into an astonishing array of convincing characters. I'd seen him become a horse groom and clergyman in the matter of the adventuress Irene Adler on behalf of the king of Bohemia, a hobo to solve the case of the Norwood builder, an opium addict in the extraordinary adventure of the man with the twisted lip, the Irish-American agent Altamont, and even a dying Sherlock Holmes to trap the poisoner Culverton Smith. In the case of the *Sign of the Four,* he so impressed Inspector Athelney Jones with a proper workhouse cough that the Scotland Yarder declared, "You would have made an actor and a rare one."

Yet none of these roles exceeded his performances that evening in a tent at the front in France as he assumed the personas of Shakespeare's melancholic Danish prince, a tormented king in what superstitious actors called "the Scottish play," Malvolio, Marc Antony making his famous funeral speech in *Julius Caesar,* and Romeo to Mrs. Morris's Juliet. But it was as Gaunt in *The Tragedy of King Richard II* that Holmes, with a curtain of army blankets as background, brought the soldiers leaping to their feet in an ovation with:

> *This happy breed of men, this little world,*
> *This precious stone set in the silver sea.*
> *Which serves it in the office of a wall,*
> *Or as a moat defensive to a house.*
> *Against the envy of less happier lands,*
> *This blessed plot, this earth, this realm, this England.*

Observing Holmes leave the makeshift platform from my vantage point offstage, I was left aghast by the unmistakable crack of a gunshot.

Grabbing Holmes, I exclaimed, "Good Lord, are you all right?"

"Yes, but that was a close one. The bullet just missed me."

"Who on earth would want to shoot you?"

"It's more likely, I think, that the shot was intended for Maitland Morris."

"Why should anyone want to kill an actor?"

"All I know at the moment is that the shot came from outside the tent and behind me. Do you see the hole that it made in the fabric of the blanket? Whoever it was, aimed at my shadow cast by the spotlight on the tent. I heard the bullet go past my head and then a splintering sound, so the bullet must have struck one of the tent supports. Yes, see there, where a hole has been gouged into the wood of that post? Do you have your trusty pocket knife?"

What appeared to me be an ordinary-looking slug from a revolver was, Holmes said after he studied it, a bullet that could only have been fired from a German Luger pistol.

"If that's true," I said urgently, "it has to have been fired by a German agent. But why would he want to kill Maitland Morris?"

"You'll have the answer to that very interesting question, Watson, when we have a talk with the missing Mr. Morris's leading lady. I'm sure you'll agree with me that Cynthia Morris is a remarkable woman, although obviously a foolishly devoted one, as is the unhappy case with so many wives of famous men."

"After all these years," I said with a chuckle, "you remain distrustful of the fair sex, eh?"

"I hope in this case," Holmes replied as we strode toward Mrs. Morris's dressing room, "that the woman is not beyond redemption! It would be a terrible loss for the theater if she were to be hanged for treason."

Judging by the worried expression on Mrs. Morris's face when Holmes and I entered her dressing room, she recognized that whatever she had done had become known. Confirmation of this came when Holmes demanded, "You know why your husband is missing. Why keep up this pretense any longer? We both know that he is a spy, or at least a German sympathizer."

Mrs. Morris rose indignantly from her dressing table. "How dare you say that?"

"Because it's true. The Foreign Office has been suspicious of him for some time. His own brother knew it. That's why he asked to have me sent up here to keep any eye on him."

As if she were a marionette whose strings had been cut, the actress sank back into her chair. "It is true," she sobbed. "God forgive him, it's true!"

"Tell us about it."

"You see, Maitland was a disciple of Houston Stewart Chamberlain."

"Who is he?" I asked. "I've never heard of this Chamberlain person."

"He is an Englishman and racist philosopher who married a daughter of the composer Richard Wagner," said Holmes, "and carried on correspondence with Kaiser Wilhelm, became a German citizen, and turned into an archenemy of England."

"I tried to reason with Maitland," Mrs. Morris continued tearfully. "I implored him to consider his British heritage, his brother's name and mine. But Maitland was a strange man. His life was one of frustration and envy. When Stanley was knighted, it hurt Maitland terribly. He said it was typical that the English would knight a soldier and yet leave a great artist such as him unrecognized, while in Berlin they really understood and rewarded the artist."

"I don't understand, Holmes," I said. "If the authorities knew all this. I'm amazed that they allowed him to come so close to the front lines at a time like this."

"It was at the general's request," Mrs. Morris replied. "He wanted to plead with him, to warn him that his secret was known, but now Maitland has gone over to the German lines."

"This is disastrous," I exclaimed. "He can give them information on the strength of our troops. He knows the password! He might even know the hour of tomorrow's attack."

Holmes inquired, "How did your husband expect to enter the German lines in safety?"

"He speaks German fluently. His pass through the German lines is the page in his book of autographs with an inscription and signature by Field Marshal von Taupnitz."

"Yes, of course. Have you told the general that his brother has gone?"

"I wasn't able to. Stanley went up to the front line immediately after the performance. But I had warned what I believed Maitland was planning to do. I thought Maitland intended to give the first performance, then cross the line afterwards. Something must have caused him to change his mind. Perhaps he suspected that I might warn the general. When I got back to our quarters, I found him gone."

I asked, "Did he leave you a note?"

"Yes. I have it here."

Taking it, Holmes read aloud, " 'I have gone, my dear. Try to understand and forgive, if you can. You wouldn't come with me, and so I am taking what is left of my heart and my hopes where they belong, among the friends that understand and appreciate me. It is something stronger than love and blood and country that makes me do this. It is something dearer to me than life itself.' "

"How could he?" cried Mrs. Morris. "Mr. Holmes, will you break the news to Stanley? I know it's cowardly of me, but I just can't bring myself to tell him."

"We'll leave at once," said Holmes. "As painful as this has been for you, dear lady, you have done the right thing and I'm sure your countrymen, and the government, will be grateful."

As we waited to see General Morris at his forward command post bunker, I was again aware of the eerie silence that continued to envelop an area that I knew would erupt at the first glimmer of dawn into the maelstrom of warfare as our army launched its attack. But as I thought about the strange silence, it occurred to me that the enemy guns might have ceased their firing because the Germans knew of Maitland Morris's plan to make his way across No Man's Land to their lines.

When I expressed this possibility to Holmes, he replied, "Undoubtedly."

"If that's so, what I don't understand is why a German agent would try to shoot him?"

At that moment, the general stepped from his bunker.

"I have bad news, Sir Stanley," announced Holmes. "Your brother has gone over."

"It's my fault. I should have put him under an armed guard, but I thought that I could reason with him, appeal to his sense of honor."

"Instead of which," said Holmes, "you tried to shoot him! But fortunately for me, you missed."

"Fortunately for you? What do you mean?"

"It was my shadow you shot at on the stage, General. When his wife informed me he'd disappeared, I took his place."

"Just a minute, Holmes," I objected. "You said the bullet that missed you was fired from a German pistol."

"It was that bullet that convinced me it had been fired by General Morris, using the very Luger pistol that's now in the holster he's wearing. I observed it when we were first introduced."

"General, are you asking me to believe," I exclaimed, "that you intended to kill your own brother? This is astounding!"

"Yes, and I'm sorry that I failed. I'd rather see Maitland dead than alive and dishonored as a traitor to his country. But now that he's become one, heaven knows what secrets he may be imparting. One thing we can be certain of is that we'll have lost the element of surprise in the attack we've planned for tomorrow."

"Possibly not, sir," said Holmes.

"What do you mean?"

"When your brother reaches enemy lines, he is the one who will be surprised. During a walk that I took around your head-quarters this evening while he and Mrs. Morris were looking at the stage I entered their quarters and altered his credentials extensively. I had been informed by my brother Mycroft of his German sympathies and the probability that he would attempt to go over to them during his visit to the front."

"Amazing, Holmes," I said. "You knew all along that Maitland Morris was a traitor."

"Therefore," Holmes continues, "I took the liberty of altering his autograph book. I have it in my pocket. I believe you will find in it a code concealed among the signatures containing valuable government information. I also switched his military travel permit with my own."

"What was the purpose of that?"

"I surmised that if he did go over, his welcome might be less cordial if the Germans had the impression that they'd captured Sherlock Holmes."

It was several weeks later that Mycroft Holmes informed us that he had learned from one of his agents in Berlin of the execution by firing squad of a man identified by the German government as an English spy by the name of Sherlock Holmes. In order to spare Cynthia Morris the embarrassment of having her husband's ignominious treason revealed, the War Office gave out a statement to the press that Maitland Morris had mistakenly entered No Man's Land and been killed during the artillery barrage that commenced the next day's attack.

With the Allied offensive underway, Holmes and I returned to London. As we said our farewell to one another on a platform at Victoria Station, my mind was full of memories of many other railway terminals as we departed or returned from one adventure or another that so often began with Holmes exclaiming, "Come, Watson! The game is afoot!"

"I have no doubt about the outcome of this war," said Holmes as we waited for his train to Sussex. "Germany will be defeated, but it will not happen until the sleeping giant of the New World rouses itself from temporary blindness to come to the rescue of the Old."

"Sleeping giant of the New World? Ah! You refer to the United States!"

"You'll recall, I trust, that I once expressed my belief that the folly of a monarch and the blundering of Parliament in far-gone years would not prevent Englishmen and Americans from being some day citizens of the same worldwide country under a flag which shall be a quartering of the Union Jack with the Stars and Stripes. I am convinced that this war will bring about that union of two great peoples that are bound together by the noble language of Shakespeare and the Bible, and that together they shall fashion a new world order in which no country will again dare to wage war upon its neighbors."

"I pray you're right, Holmes."

"I fear that if it doesn't happen as a result of this war," he said as he struck a match to light a pipe, "within twenty years England and her American cousins may again be required to rally and unite against an even greater threat to civilization."

With that, he settled into the carriage that would carry him back to his rustic retirement and contemplation of the culture of bees. I climbed into a cab to take me to my medical practice in Harley Street.

· 2 ·

The Paradol Chamber

In the seven years following my introduction to Sherlock Holmes in the chemistry lab of St. Bart's hospital in 1881 by our mutual acquaintance, young Stamford, resulting in Holmes and I agreeing to share lodgings in Baker Street, I had grown accustomed to his investigations that began with the arrival of an urgent telegram or the plodding footsteps of a Scotland Yard official ascending the stairs with a grudging appeal for assistance. On several occasions, a case started with the unexpected arrival at our door of someone desperately seeking the intervention of the world's first private consulting detective.

It was on such an unanticipated instance that I met the remarkable woman who was to become my first wife. Seeking

Holmes's assistance at the suggestion of a former beneficiary of Holmes's unique profession, Mary Morstan entered the sitting room that also served as Holmes's consulting chamber with a firm step and calm composure. She was a small, dainty blonde, well gloved and dressed in the most perfect taste. Her purpose in calling upon Holmes, she explained, concerned the mysterious disappearance three years earlier in London of her father. A captain of the Thirty-Fourth Bombay Infantry, he had been one of the officers in charge of prisoners in the remote and desolate Andaman Islands of the Indian Ocean.

Since her father had vanished, Miss Morstan continued, she had received a package in the post on the same date each year containing a large and lustrous pearl without any clue as to the sender. On the day that she called upon Holmes, she had received a letter stating that she was a wronged woman deserving of justice. The sender requested that she be at the third pillar from the left outside the Lyceum Theater that evening. It stated that she could bring two friends, so long as they were not the police. Holmes agreed that he and I would accompany her.

When Miss Morstan departed, I watched her from a window as she walked briskly down Baker Street. When she was no longer in view, I turned to Holmes and exclaimed, "What a very attractive woman!"

"Is she? I did not observe."

In response to my retort that he could be outrageously inhuman at times, he remained perfectly calm. He explained the necessity in his profession of not allowing his judgment to be biased by the personal traits of a client and stated that emotional qualities were antagonistic to clear reasoning.

My notebooks are replete with his observations and dark

opinions on the subject of the gentler sex. On one occasion, he confessed that the female heart and the feminine mind were insoluble puzzles to him. Murder might be condoned or explained, but a smaller offense would rankle. His abiding conviction was that women were never entirely to be trusted, not the best of them. As evidence he pointed out that the most winning woman he ever knew had poisoned her three children for their insurance money. Of the numerous challenging cases that he undertook, he grudgingly admitted to having been bested three times by women. The most remarkable of them was the opera singer and adventuress of dubious and questionable memory named Irene Adler. After the affair that I recorded concerning a potential scandal over an indiscretion by the king of Bohemia, Holmes referred to her with both disdain and admiration as *the* woman.

The mystery presented by Miss Morstan, which I recorded in detail as the case of the *Sign of the Four,* involved several murders, deceit, treachery, betrayal, the fabulous Agra Treasure, a one-legged man, and a hideous creature from the Andamans named Tonga. By the end of this unique adventure I found myself in love with Miss Morstan and thrilled when she accepted my proposal of marriage. Unable to bring himself to offer me congratulations, Holmes said, "I should never marry, lest it bias my judgment."

The immediate consequence of my wedding and the obligations of matrimony was that I was no longer able to assist the man who had so often proven to be the last court of appeal for people of all kinds and from all strata of life, from the lowest ranks of society to royalty, as well as the official police, who found themselves in need of help. A happier result of marriage was that I was able to take over the thriving medial practice of a friend who had chosen to retire. This purchase was made possible with Mary's financial assistance. In addition to the sale of the pearls that had been sent to her as a means of affording her justice in the murder of her father, she had been provided a substantial dowry by Thaddeus Sholto, the conscience-stricken son of Major John Sholto, a principal in the Agra Treasure affair.

On a particularly cold and blustery evening a few months after my marriage, as I was at my desk in the corner of our cheery parlor and going over the family account book, Mary was seated by the fire and stitching away at a piece of embroidery. Looking toward me, she said, "John, dear, don't look so troubled."

Setting side the ledger, I asked, "Oh? Was I looking troubled?"

"You've been scowling at that book for ten minutes now. What's the matter, dear. Aren't the figures adding up correctly?"

"In fact, they tell a very pretty story. I find we have nearly a hundred and fifty pounds. I was thinking that because we don't need the money just now, we might invest it. In something really sound, of course."

"Do you have anything in mind?"

"Peruvian silver! I bumped into Dr. Wilson during my rounds at Saint Bart's hospital this morning. He told me that his investment in it has provided a handsome return and that he can put me in touch with his broker. What do you think of the idea?"

Laying aside her needlework, she smiled mischievously. "I've also been giving thought to making a business investment."

"Really? What sort of business?"

"While you were making your rounds yesterday, a most charming man called here at the suggestion of Mrs. Cecil Forrester to speak to me about buying stock in his new company. He was so enthusiastic about its prospects that I told him I would discuss the matter with you. It is a manufacturing firm that has the rights to a wonderful new type of metal discovered by a brilliant young chemist in America. He left a prospectus. I put it in the right hand drawer of your desk."

The lavishly printed brochure offering Paradol Preferred Stock described "an amazing new metal discovered by Dr. Paradene." Claiming "immeasurable potentialities" of the alloy, it continued with the astonishing assertions that the fourth dimension had been conquered and that something it termed "spacial dislocation" had become an accomplished fact.

"Good gracious me, my dear," I exclaimed as I tossed the document into the waste bin, "this is absolute poppycock. There is no such thing as the fourth dimension. This company is an outright fraud."

"As I recall, that's what everyone said about the telephone! There must be something to this. The gentleman who left the prospectus invited me to visit the firm's laboratory to witness a demonstration by Dr. Paradene. He insisted that I bring you along. I agreed to do so. We are to be at the laboratory at ten o'clock tomorrow morning."

The address of the Paradol company given to Mary was a small building in an industrial section of the East End near the spot on the Thames where Holmes apprehended Jonathan Small in the affair of the *Sign of the Four*. We were admitted to the building by a tall, thin man with a receding hairline, gaunt face, and small snakelike eyes. "Dr. Paradene will be with you both in a moment," he said. "She is just concluding an experiment."

"What's that?" I exclaimed. "Dr. Paradene is a woman?"

"Yes, sir," said the man as he withdrew, "and quite a brilliant one."

"That's the last straw," said I to Mary. "The whole thing sounded like a fraud, and now we get here and find that a woman doctor is at the back of it all."

"Really, John. That is a remark I'd expect to hear from Sherlock Holmes."

At that moment, a door opened and a dark-haired young woman wearing a white smock introduced herself as Dr. Paradene. "I'm so glad you've come," she said. "Please step into my laboratory."

Before us as we entered stood a large metal box. About the size of a prison cell, it had a solid door with a sliding panel that opened to reveal a small, square peep hole covered by metal screening. Next to this entrance was an array of switches and dials. "This chamber is made of large sheets of my new alloy that have been welded to form the walls, ceiling, and floor," said the doctor. "When the door is shut and the viewing portal is closed, it is completely sealed."

"What's its purpose? Do people get inside it?"

"If they do when the machine is turned on, they're liable to find themselves transported many miles from here. But at the moment there is no danger of that happening, so please step in with me and examine the interior."

The chamber reminded me of a walk-in bank vault at the firm of Cox and Company in Charing Cross where I kept an old ammunition box containing my notes on several of Holmes's cases that were too sensitive to be published while those who had been involved were sill alive.

"Feel free to examine the room," said the doctor. "You will find the walls are solid and air tight."

This proved true. I found the chamber's walls, floor, and ceiling seamless.

As we stepped from the box, Dr. Paradene summoned the

man who had greeted us upon our arrival. "This is Albert, my assistant," she explained. "With his help, I shall demonstrate the workings of the machine."

With that, Albert entered the chamber, and Dr. Paradene closed and locked the door. A moment later, she threw a switch that activated an electrical generator.

"In a few seconds," she said as the machinery hummed, "Albert will be gone."

"Scientifically impossible," I muttered.

"Permit me to explain, Dr. Watson. The metal alloy that I have named Paradol causes a dislocation in the warp of space that enables us to enter the fourth dimension. Combined with the great force of electricity, it results in the transformation of an object's molecular structure so that the object can be transmitted to another place in much the same manner that the telephone carries the human voice. I call this new force 'teleportation.' "

Turning off the mechanism, she opened the door to reveal an empty chamber.

"It's a trick," I exclaimed. "This room has a hidden means of exit."

"Perhaps another demonstration will serve to dispel your doubts. May I propose one which does not involve a human being? I suggest that we use the small parcel with the brown wrapping paper on the table by the door. It contains copies of the Paradol prospectus. To assure you that there is no trickery, I suggest that you put your initials on it."

Inscribing "J H W" on the package, I asked, "Shall I write my address?"

"That won't be necessary," she said. After taking the parcel and placing it on the floor of the chamber, she closed the door to the box and switched on the electricity. A moment later, she shut down the machine and opened the chamber door.

"It's not there, John," said Mary excitedly. "The package is gone!"

"You'll find it waiting for you," replied Dr. Paradene, "when you return to your house."

To my astonishment upon our arrival at our home about an hour later, Mary and I found the parcel with my initials on it lying on the doorstep. As a man of reason, I could provide no explanation for what I had observed, except that Paradene had discovered in the alloy she called Paradol a means of transporting matter from one place to another. Yet, being a man of science, I found myself unable to accept that anything could be taken apart, transmitted through a fourth dimension, and perfectly reassembled elsewhere. As I pondered the possibility that Dr. Paradene had actually achieved this, I recalled that on countless occasions I had heard Sherlock Holmes pronounce his maxim that when you have eliminated the impossible, whatever remains, however improbable, must be the truth. But he also had frequently lectured me that there is nothing more deceptive than an obvious fact. Accordingly, I decided that before I yielded to Mary's desire to invest in Paradene's venture, it would be prudent to go to Baker Street and lay out for Homes the events that Mary and I had witnessed in the Paradol Chamber.

From time to time since I moved out of 221B Baker Street, I heard accounts of Holmes's doings. They included a summons to Odessa in the case of the Trepov murder and his clearing up the singular tragedy of the Atkinson brothers. In a few instances, I read between the lines of reports in newspapers of an arrest or sensational achievement claimed by Scotland

Yarders and discerned the behind-the-scenes hand of my old friend.

It felt like old times when Mrs. Hudson opened the door of my former lodgings, but as I stepped into the foyer, she exclaimed, "Thank goodness you're here, doctor. I'm worried about Mr. Holmes. He's been shut up in his rooms for three days now with the window shades drawn and the door locked. He won't even open it for me when I bring him his food. I think he's been living on tins of biscuits."

"Great scot," I replied as I rushed up the stairs.

Several loud knocks on the door elicited, "Who is it?"

"Watson!"

"What is your middle name?"

"You know very well that it's Hamish."

"And your wife's maiden name?"

"Mary Morstan. Really, Holmes, this is ridiculous."

"It is not ridiculous," said Holmes as he opened the door, "when Professor Moriarty has decided that it's high time he settled his score with me."

"What do you mean?"

"He has sent his minions to kill me several times. Twice, I've been attacked in the streets, and only yesterday a shot was fired through the window behind you."

"Have you informed the police?"

"Our friends at Scotland Yard," said Holmes as he took a pipe from the rack he kept on the mantle, "remain unconvinced that the Napoleon of Crime exists. But this little matter is of no concern to you, my friend. Occupy your old chair, and tell me the details of the crisis that's brought you around in such a state of urgency that you felt the necessity to leave your medical practice in the evening when you are customarily the busiest."

"I wouldn't call it a crisis," I replied. "I'm motivated by caution and curiosity."

"Admirable traits, my good fellow."

"Have you ever heard of a new metal called Paradol and its inventor, Dr. Paradene?"

"Yes indeed. I received a prospectus concerning it the other day."

"What do you think of it?"

"It's obviously rubbish designed to fool a gullible public into buying shares. Don't tell me that you were taken in by it?"

"No, of course not. Naturally, as a scientific man I knew it was rubbish. However, my wife got a bit involved in the concern, and so today to prove to her that the whole thing was a fraud, I went to the laboratory and met this Dr. Paradene. The doctor is a woman, by the way! We stayed long enough to observe a demonstration of what she calls teleportation."

After hearing my account of what had transpired concerning the parcel that appeared on our doorstep, Holmes took a final puff of his pipe and said, "A childish trick. Obviously, this Paradol Chamber contains an ingeniously hidden trap door through which the assistant, James, disappeared with the package containing your initials, took a fast cab and delivered it to your home well before you could get there."

"I tried to tell Mary that the whole thing was a fraud, but you know how women are. She was very obstinate, so I hoped that you would help me expose it."

"For your sake, old fellow, I'll be glad to do anything I can."

"I thought we might go to the laboratory late tonight when no one is there and take a look at that Paradol Chamber a little more closely."

"Good idea, Watson. After being cooped up here for three

days, it will be a pleasure to get some night air and indulge in a little simple burglarizing."

"Shall I call for you here?"

"Much too dangerous. I'll be in a hansom cab outside your house about eleven-thirty tonight. How's that?"

"Splendid. It will be quite like old times."

A clock in a bell tower was striking midnight as we approached the laboratory. Finding the door locked, Holmes drew a pocket burglary kit that he'd used with excellent effect to enter the house of the blackmailer Charles Augustus Milverton. In the case of the retired colourman, he bragged about his skill as a cracksman, stating, "Burglary has always been an alternative profession had I cared to adopt it, and I have little doubt that I should have come to the front."

Observing the Paradol Chamber in the soft light from a lantern that he'd brought, Holmes remarked, "It's quite an elaborate contraption,"

Finding the chamber's door had been left open, I proposed that we go in.

"Not both of us, Watson," said Holmes. "If this is the only entrance, and the two of us walked in, it would be too easy for someone to slam the door shut on us. You stay out here and keep watch. But I trust that I won't find myself suddenly teleported to your doorstep."

"Very funny, Holmes," said I, nervously.

Moments after entering the chamber with burglary kit in hand, Holmes shouted, "There's a woman's body! She's been shot and has been dead several hours."

Rushing inside, I blurted, "Good Lord. It's Dr. Paradene.

Looking up with an expression of alarm, Holmes shouted, "Watson, get out of here!"

At that moment, the chamber door slammed shut and its lock snapped closed.

"I should have anticipated this," Holmes declared. "We've walked into a Moriarty trap. I ought to have deduced a scheme designed to lure me with an intriguing problem in which the victim was the wife of my oldest and best friend and chronicler of my adventures in crime. You knew it would get back to my ears, didn't you, Moriarty?"

As Holmes shone the lantern light on the door, the cover of the peephole slid back and a man's voice said, "You have indeed been trapped, Mr. Holmes. The Paradol Chamber will soon be your coffin. It is, as Dr. Watson can attest, airtight. Once I close this cover, you will begin to consume all of the oxygen. It will be a slow death, of course, in which you will become aware of what's happening. My only regret is that you will be accompanied by Dr. Watson into what Will Shakespeare called the bourne from which no one returns. That was not my intention. Despite your slavish admiration for Holmes, Doctor, I've actually become quite fond of you."

"Blast you, Moriarty," I railed. "You are a fiend, and I have no doubt that one day you will reap your just dessert at the end of a hangman's rope in Newgate Prison!"

"I think not, sir."

"If you were so certain that we would fall into your trap, why did you find it necessary to murder Dr. Paradene?"

"I'm sure your friend Holmes will be glad to answer that query, Doctor."

"As with so many of your accomplices," said Holmes, "this woman simply outlived her usefulness. Once the trap was baited, she was not only no longer needed, but might become an inconvenient liability."

"Precisely, Holmes. But now I must close this panel and bid you good-bye."

The opening through which Moriarty had been speaking closed with a click and an awful finality. Turning to Holmes, I said, "I'm sorry I led you into this, my friend."

"Cheer up, Watson. The game's not over yet."

"I'm afraid it is. There is no way out of this chamber."

"Of course there is. You're forgetting that an exit from this room was used by the man who delivered the parcel with your initials on it to your home. All we have to do is find it."

"It's no good, Holmes. I thoroughly examined the walls of this hideous place. They are as solid as the walls around Buckingham Palace."

"If there isn't a way out of here," said Holmes, "I may find myself a believer in the idea of teleportation after all. Have you got a box of matches?"

"Of course."

"Silly question! Every man who enjoys smoking a pipe or fine cigar can be counted on to have at last one box. I always carry two. They and yours should suffice."

After he struck the first match, I immediately saw his purpose. By holding it close to the thin line between two sheets of Paradol metal that formed one section of the chamber's walls, he was hoping that a flicker of the flame would show a seepage of air through the crack, indicating the existence of a portal. When an examination of the chamber's four walls proved unavailing, he commenced an exploration of the chamber's floor. This eventually required moving the body of the dead woman.

After lighting the fifth match of his search and seeing it go out, Holmes bolted out of his crouch. "Success at last, Watson," he exclaimed. "There was purpose in Moriarty placing the body in this spot. This misguided woman was killed and her body placed here in order to hide the means of exit from this hellish room. There may have been a device used by the man named James to open it during the demonstrations you witnessed, but fortunately, we have my burglary kit. If you will bring it to me, there is a very handy chisel in it that is exactly the tool to pry open the trapdoor."

Again exhibiting his dexterity with such implements, Holmes quickly had the trapdoor open, revealing a ladder that descended to a narrow tunnel. While he went down into it with the lantern, I remained in the darkness of the hideous chamber that Moriarty had constructed with the anticipation of making it the tomb of Mr. Sherlock Holmes. But my feeling of exultation that Moriarty's evil scheming had again been thwarted was dashed as Holmes reappeared and said, "I'm sorry to disappoint you, but Moriarty left nothing to chance. Our exit has been closed by a freshly built brick wall. I tried smashing through it, but the mortar has become firmly set. All we can do now is try to conserve the air in this room. Because, as you well know, the human body in sleep consumes less oxygen, I suggest we settle down as comfortably as possible for the night."

"If it's our time to die," I said, "I'm glad that we are together again, although it was my stupidity that led you into this mess."

"Be of good cheer, my friend," Holmes responded as he extinguished the lantern, "and remember the old adage that it always seems darkest before the dawn."

In a fitful sleep upon the hard floor, I alternately dreamed of exciting adventures shared with Holmes and scenes of domestic bliss in the company of my darling wife. When I finally awoke, I found that Holmes had lit the lantern and was standing by the chamber door, looking remarkably composed.

"What I wouldn't give," I said as I rose from the floor, "to have one of Mrs. Hudson's magnificent breakfasts right now. Or to hear the heavy tread of Inspector Lestrade on the stairs."

"What about the sound of the feet of the intrepid boys of the unofficial police force by the name of the Baker Street Irregulars?"

With a grunt, I replied, "Even them!"

"I can't promise you a proper breakfast, my friend, but you may get your wish concerning the Irregulars."

"What do you mean?"

"They are a reliable band of boys, able to go anywhere, see all, and overhear everyone. That is why I engaged them to follow and observe me last evening, with instructions that if I did not leave this building after two hours, they were to go to Scotland Yard and fetch Lestrade."

"In this instance, your confidence in them seems to have been misplaced."

"It is strange that they haven't appeared by now," said Holmes glumly. "They have never let me down. You must concede that they did extraordinary work in locating the steam launch *Aurora* in the Jonathan Small matter."

Resigned to our fate, we both fell silent and remained so for a long time.

Feeling increasingly somnolent, I was abruptly roused by a clamor outside the Paradol Chamber. Leaping to his feet, Holmes declared, "I believe rescue is at hand, Watson!"

An instant later, the chamber door was flung wide open and I found myself gazing in amazement at Inspector Lestrade, a group of policemen in uniform, and a beloved face I had believed I would never see again.

"It's all right, John," said Mary as she rushed to embrace me. "Be assured I shall never again suggest an investment!"

"You see, Watson," said Holmes, "the Irregulars came through and brought Lestrade."

"The only thing I know about those ragamuffins," retorted the inspector with his usual look of befuddlement, "is that a report was filed stating they'd been found tied up not far from here by an officer making his rounds. It was Mrs. Watson who came to me this morning seeking the assistance of my office."

Beaming with pride, I said, "You, Mary?"

"When you left home in the company of Mr. Holmes and did not return by this morning," she explained, "I knew something was terribly wrong, so I sought out the inspector and told him about the Pardaol Chamber and of my suspicion that you and Mr. Holmes had come here."

"There you have it," said Holmes. "The initiative shown by your devoted wife has proven my maxim that the intuition of a woman may be more valuable than the conclusion drawn by an analytical reasoner."

· 3 ·

The Accidental Murderess

*L*ate on a beautiful summer morning in 1895, Sherlock Holmes arose from his bed to find me engaged in reviewing my notes on a case that had taken us to the Vatican at the request of His Holiness the Pope to settle the delicate matter of the death of Cardinal Cosca. We'd returned to London from Rome at a very late hour the previous evening. Because Holmes was customarily a late riser, except when an investigation was afoot, I had not expected him to be up and about for several more hours.

"Well, well," he said as he chose a pipe from an array of black bent briars on the mantle. "I see that my Boswell is striking while the literary iron is still hot. I trust that your account of our Italian excursion will not result in yet another overly romanticized chronicle that puts the emphasis on the sensational aspects, while rendering scant attention to the instruction of your readers about the science of deduction. Have you had breakfast?"

"Several hours ago."

"After three days of Italian cuisine," he declared, "I'm longing for incomparable English fare as only our landlady can prepare it."

After a tug on the bell rope to summon Mrs. Hudson, he proceeded to fill the pipe with the tobacco he kept in the toe of a Persian slipper.

"In going over my notes," I said, "I find there's one thing in this matter of Cardinal Cosca that you haven't explained."

"Is that so? I thought I'd covered everything in detail on the voyage home," he replied as he sank into his favorite chair. "What is it that I appear to have omitted?"

"At what point did you suspect that Fascetti was a member of Garibaldi's revolutionary Red Shirts and was masquerading as a brother of the Franciscan Order?"

"I noticed immediately that he had looped the sash of his robe the wrong way round."

"You never fail to amaze me," I said with a chuckle. "A little thing like that led you to the solution of a puzzle that might have shaken the very foundations of the papacy!"

"You know that my entire career has been built on the observation of the little things," he said through a puff of smoke. "For example, I deduce from the handbill that lies amidst other material on your desk that you appear to be contemplating an excursion to Warwickshire to take in the annual festival at the birthplace of the Bard of Avon. It's a capital idea. Nothing restores the soul and reinvigorates the spirit quite as well as immersion in all the glories of England's, and therefore the world's greatest playwright. Because of your exertions in Italy, you've earned a respite in the refreshing air of Stratford-upon-Avon."

"If anyone is deserving of a vacation, it's you. Come with me! Such a change of pace will do you a world of good."

In expressing this opinion I expected to hear a lecture on Holmes's aversion to leaving London that he enunciated in a case that had taken us to a rural estate named Copper Beeches. "It is my belief," he stated on that occasion, "that the lowest and vilest alleys in London do not represent a more dreadful record of sin that does the smiling and beautiful countryside."

Where I saw lovely old houses, he envisioned them obscuring deeds of hellish cruelty and hidden wickedness. But as I anticipated a rejection of my suggestion, he asked, "How long do you expect you'll be away?"

"The festival runs two weeks."

"Good Lord. It lasts an entire fortnight?"

"The program is an extensive one. It runs the gamut from *The Tempest* to *Othello* and includes *Twelfth Night,* in which you had your triumph as Malvolio while touring America with the Sasanoff Company in your youth. If that's not enticement enough, one of the performers is the most promising Shakespearean actor of the day."

"Dennis Romney will be there?"

"I've never seen you so impressed, Holmes."

"Mr. Romney is an impressive artist. His portrayal of King Lear last season was truly astonishing. Very well, old friend, you've persuaded me. I'll be delighted to accompany you."

As I contemplated our holiday and Holmes feasted on Mrs. Hudson's breakfast, I had no idea that he and I were about to commence an adventure that was a recipe consisting of equal parts of the beautiful English countryside and black villainy, mixed with a dash of romance and a sprinkling of danger seasoned with theatrical condiments. It was to be an adventure that nearly cost Holmes his life.

In the first week of the outing, we enjoyed days of exploring the modest house where Shakespeare had resided, the Ann Hathaway cottage and other interesting landmarks. Evenings were passed at the theater. On Tuesday of the second week, we decided to go for a walk through the nearby Avon Forest. Holmes appeared in remarkable high spirits with a twinkle in his eyes as he said, "Watson, for once I begin to wish that I were a man of wealth. Seeing the beauty of this place, I am perfectly certain that I'd be happy in retirement here. It's rather depressing to think that in just a few days the sordid necessity of making money will demand my return to Baker Street and re-entry into a world of criminals."

"Yes, in surroundings like these it is a little hard to think of crime."

Our idyllic walk had brought us to a turn of the path that would have taken us down a steep slope toward the River Avon, and we were pausing to take in the lovely view through a space between the lush foliage of the woods, when the quiet was shattered by an explosion.

"Great scot," I exclaimed, " I believe that was the blast of a rifle."

As I turned toward Holmes, I discovered him staggering backward. Grimacing with pain, he gasped, "I'm afraid I'm hurt, Watson."

Rushing to examine him, I exclaimed, "Badly? Where is the wound?"

Clutching his left arm, he answered calmly, "My shoulder."

"Your sleeve is soaked with blood. Can you get out of your coat?"

"I'm sure it's superficial. I'm more interested in finding out from what direction the shot came. If it struck a tree and we can find it, we should be able to deduce where it was fired from. By the way, did you notice that the shot sounded unusually loud and that it produced a curious echo?"

While he examined several trees, I ventured, "Surely, this was accidental, an errant shot by a rabbit hunter, perhaps."

"Possibly," he muttered as he studied a gouge in the trunk of an oak that must have been there in Shakespeare's time. Using a jackknife that I always carried, he soon dug out a badly disfigured bullet. "However," he said, examining it, "I find it difficult to see how a tall man in an Inverness cloak and a deerstalker cap could be easily mistaken for a woodland creature with short legs and long ears, even at the considerable distance from which this bullet was fired."

Brushing aside my plea to examine him and a demand that we immediately return to the village for treatment of his wound, he aligned the location where the bullet ended up and the place where he'd been standing and determined that it had to have been discharged from a small clump of trees at the edge of a clearing about halfway along the gently sloping path that led down to the riverside.

"The topography is certainly interesting," said Holmes as we started down the hillside, "not to mention the fascinating matter of the bullet's trajectory."

We'd traveled only a short distance when we observed a man and woman hurrying up the hill. Of middle age, he had the distinguished bearing of a country gentleman. Much younger, she was quite attractive. Dressed in hunting attire, each carried a rifle. As they approached, the man shouted, "Was anyone hurt?"

"Yes indeed," I yelled. "My friend's been wounded in the shoulder!"

"Oh how dreadful," said the woman breathlessly as they arrived. "It was an accident that was my fault. I am terribly sorry."

"How did it happen?" I demanded.

The obviously distraught gentleman replied anxiously, "We were out rabbit shooting. I was teaching my wife to use a rifle."

"I saw a rabbit scurrying across the clearing," the woman interjected. "I raised the rifle and fired, but as I did so Geoffrey jolted my arm."

"Yes, I'm afraid I did, Alice," said he excitedly. "I was also going to shoot, but when I lifted my gun, I bumped your elbow and sent your shot wild. I can't tell you how sorry I am, sir. Of course, we'll take care of any expenses."

At that moment, Holmes swayed against me and sank to the ground in a faint.

Fortunately, the hunters had come to the site of this terrible happenstance in a riding trap that served nicely in getting Holmes back to Stratford-upon-Avon and into a hospital. Although the wound to his shoulder proved not serious, he had bled profusely. With the injury treated and bandaged, I accompanied the nurses as they took him to a recovery room. When they were gone, Holmes looked up at me and inquired, "Are we alone, Watson?"

"For the moment."

"Where are the man and his wife?"

"Downstairs in the waiting room. Their names are Geoffrey

and Alice Markham. They are terribly upset about what happened and have invited me to luncheon with them to receive a report on you condition."

Startling me by sitting up, he said, "Now that we're alone I can stop pretending that I'm at death's door and knocking!"

"Are you telling me," I said remonstrated, "that your fainting spell was a sham?"

"It was a necessary ruse, old fellow."

"To what purpose?"

"As chronicler of fifteen years of my cases, you surely must have observed that among the several faculties that have contributed to my successes in the field of crime detection is that I never forget a face. The moment we encountered this woman calling herself Mrs. Alice Markham, I recognized her. And I'm certain that she recognized me at once. That is why it is vitally important that she assume I'm out of action for awhile. She is in reality the notorious Mrs. Dangerfield. Do you recall the case?"

Because I was recently married at the time and therefore not involved in his investigation of that affair, I followed developments in the newspapers. "As I recall," said I, "she was tried for the murder of her husband by poisoning."

"It was I who tracked down the sale of the arsenic that she claimed to have purchased for cosmetic purposes," Holmes continued. "She was acquitted because the jurors were informed through testimony in her defense that her husband had been addicted to arsenic. They accepted the explanation of the defense counsel that he'd accidentally taken an overdose."

"If this woman was exonerated, why should she attempt to kill you?"

"There are two possible explanations. The first and easier is continuing resentment over my investigation and testimony given at her trial."

"Revenge!"

"More likely is that she learned of my presence at the festival and fears that I may be looking into the circumstances of the previous death of her wealthy uncle. He was killed in a shooting on a grouse moor in Scotland. She was a member of the hunting party and benefited from his demise in the form of a substantial fortune."

"If this woman has committed two murders," I exclaimed, "she gives new meaning to the term *femme fatale.*"

"Indeed so, my friend. She is one of the most dangerous women I've ever encountered. That is why you must tread carefully in dealing with her."

"In dealing with her? What do you mean?"

"I'm certain that she will want to know as much as possible about the prognosis for my recovery. When you have lunch with the Markhams, tell her that I will have to be hospitalized for several days and then return to London for a long period of recuperation. Then keep an eye on her. Find out as much as you can and report back to me."

To my surprise and pleasure, I found that Mrs. Markham had invited the actor Dennis Romney to join us for lunch at the couple's very old house at the edge of Stratford-upon-Avon. She explained that because she was interested in taking up acting herself, Mr. Romney had been coaching her and felt she exhibited such promise that he would recommend her for small roles during the next year's festival.

Although I expressed delight at the prospect of meeting the renowned thespian, Markham left no doubt prior to Mr. Romney's arrival that he did not share his wife's infatuation with the man by referring to him as "this acting fellow." As we sipped an exceptionally fine sherry, he complained, "Like all actors, he's full of himself. He's constantly quoting from Shakespeare and behaving generally as if he were another Sir Henry Irving."

Before the meal my host and the handsome young actor engaged in such sharp repartee in a verbal duel on the subject of Shakespearean dramas that I felt as though I were seated front-row-center for the final act of *Hamlet*, except for the absence of actual swords. The curtain was rung down on this contentious discussion only when Mrs. Markham turned to her husband and suggested that he not only take me on a tour of their venerable house, but show me Markham's butterfly collection.

"Have you any interest in entomology?" asked Markham as we ascended the stairway to view the repository of his hobby.

I replied that while Sherlock Homes possessed an impressive knowledge of the insect order Lepidoptera, my only experience regarding chasing, collecting, and classifying butterflies and people who engaged in it had been garnered in the matter of the Hound of the Baskervilles. "It was a devilishly interesting case," I continued, "in that it involved a most dastardly amateur practitioner of catching and preserving them by the name of Jack Stapleton."

As we reached a balcony overlooking the large parlor below and I paused by a banister to peer down at my hostess and Mr. Romney, Markham warned, "Be careful, Doctor. Don't put all your weight on that railing. It's riddled with worm holes. I have often expressed a desire to replace the wood, but my wife insists that doing so would detract from the charm of this ancient house. Are you a married man, Doctor?"

"I'm a widower. My wife passed away few months ago."

"I'm very sorry," Markham replied as he opened the door to

the room containing his butterflies. "Welcome to my modest museum! I think you'll find some of the finest specimens. I am not exaggerating when I tell you that I doubt you'll find a finer one outside the Museum of Natural History in London."

With the pride of a man who had spent years assembling the collection, he beamed as he showed me a bewildering assortment of delicate and magnificently hued examples that had been carefully preserved and mounted on cardboard in glass cases.

"When you capture a butterfly," I inquired, "how do you kill it without damaging it?"

"With poison, of course."

"Cyanide?"

"Oh no, I use arsenic."

"Really? Why? As I recall, the man I told you about, Jack Stapleton, used cyanide."

Suddenly appearing agitated, Markham retorted, "Why all this interest in my choice of poison, sir? I find your query baffling."

"I posed the question merely as a man of science."

"I find arsenic more appropriate for the purpose," he said impatiently, "because it also serves as a preservative."

After a few tense minutes of examining the collection, Markham and I returned to the ground floor and found that his wife and Mr. Romney had already gone into the dining room. As we were about to enter, we overheard Mrs. Markham say, "Geoffrey has no imagination. He's never understood me. I rue the day that I married him!"

At this singularly inopportune moment, Markham sighed deeply and whispered to me, "Well, Doctor, it's true what they say, that eavesdroppers never hear good of themselves."

"I'm truly sorry, sir"

"There are times," he said with a worried expression, "when

I see my wife with young Romney and wonder if she wouldn't like me to get out of the way."

After abiding one of the most embarrassing and painful luncheons I'd ever sat through, I returned to the hospital to report to Holmes. As always, he listened intently without interrupting my narrative. When I concluded, he asked, "What do you make of it, Watson?"

"It's a situation fraught with sinister possibilities."

"Indeed it is. But for whom?"

"Why for Markham, of course. We know that the woman is a poisoner. I was left with the impression that he also knows her dubious history."

"She got away with murder once," Holmes responded. "The question is, would she dare to try it again with poison, or might she attempt to rid herself of her husband without raising suspicions as happened with her uncle?"

"I see what your mean! The method is at hand in the rickety balcony railing. One push when he wasn't looking, and it would be the end of him. It would be put down as an accident."

"What a charming household! Your description of Markham's behavior when you asked about arsenic is interesting."

"I raised the subject to see how he would react."

"Very astute of you, old fellow. Are you amenable to seeing the Markhams again?"

"As a matter of fact, I've been invited along with Dennis Romney by Mrs. Markham to a picnic tea, followed by a boat ride on the Avon this afternoon."

"You've done splendidly."

"What about you? How are you feeling? What did the hospital surgeon's examination reveal about the severity of your wound?"

"The object that caused it is in the night stand."

Opening the drawer, I found a nearly pristine bullet and asked, "How can this be? The bullet that hit your shoulder was dug out of a tree trunk."

"The explanation is elementary. There were *two* shots fired almost simultaneously, the one that went into the tree and the other into me."

"That accounts for the unusually loud sound that we heard at the time and what seemed to be an echo."

"Exactly. It also raises the fascinating question of which bullet came from which of the Markhams' rifles. While I wrestle with this problem, I'll be relying on you to continue observing all the players in this drama during the festive afternoon outing to which you've been invited."

In retrospect, Holmes's choice of the adjective to describe the events of the remainder of the day proved to be ironic. Instead of a participating in a festive picnic and placid boat ride upon the River Avon, I found myself feeling like a one-man audience at a play that was part farce and part melodrama with a bit of histrionics and a London East End Music Hall's low slapstick thrown in for good measure.

Late that afternoon, within moments of the blanket being spread on the ground and the picnic laid out, a row erupted between the Markhams. Presumably the consequence of his pent-up resentment after overhearing his wife's cruel and sinister sentiments expressed to the actor before lunch, the vituperative exchange raged sporadically on the boat. When we were at last and mercifully making our way back to shore, the ugly exchanges had been replaced by brooding silences. I was seated alone at the prow of the smart little river craft with my back to the three of them. Hearing a splash, I turned around in state of alarm and saw that Geoffrey Markham had somehow gone overboard.

As I reached out in an attempt to fish him out of the water, he shouted angrily, "One of them pushed me!"

Both Mrs. Markham and Romney denied having done so, of course. Whether it was true or Markham had simply lost his footing was impossible for me to know. When he was back on board, he was thoroughly soaked and shivering from the cold water. Upon our return to the Markhams' house, I was concerned that he might develop a chill and insisted that he go directly to bed.

When Mrs. Markham also urged this, he snapped like a vicious dog. "I am perfectly all right," he barked, "no thanks to you and your friend Romney."

The actor shot to his feet and railed, "What do you mean by that, sir? I know you don't like me, but how dare you hurl such an accusation at Alice?"

"One of you shoved me into the water when my back was turned at a point where the river was deepest. If you don't like the way I talk to my wife, you can clear out of my house!"

Wheeling around, he stormed from the room with the assertion that he was cold and was going to fetch a scarf.

After a moment of embarrassed silence, Mrs. Markham offered me an apology for his behavior. "I really don't know what's come over Geoffrey," she said solicitously. "It started a few weeks ago with an argument about his taking out large insurance policies on both of us."

As I was about to pursue this possibly important information, the door bell rang. It was answered by Geoffrey Markham. To my astonishment and everyone else's, the caller turned out to be Sherlock Holmes.

"What a pleasant surprise," said Mrs. Markham. "I

understood from Dr. Watson that you were to remain in hospital for a few more days."

"Yes, Holmes," said I. "You shouldn't be up."

"The constitution of an ox and the obstinacy of a mule, two characteristics of mine to which Watson can attest, combined to make an early departure from the hospital possible."

"I'm glad that you're feeling better," replied Mrs. Markham. "I do hope that you'll stay for dinner."

"Thank you, I will," he replied as he turned to Romney. "How do you do, sir? I've seen you at the theater on several occasions."

Burning for an explanation of Holmes's sudden arrival, I presently managed to draw him aside and whisper an account of the disturbing events of the afternoon's singular outing. "All of that is instructive, my friend," he said in a hushed voice. "In the meantime, I myself have not been idle. I think our stage has been set for a dramatic last act curtain."

Having learned from my years of association with Holmes in the myriads of his cases that it would be pointless to press him for an explanation, I restrained my curiosity and waited for the plan he had evidently devised to unfold. Probably because of his unexpected presence, our three companions at the dinner table displayed none of their previous rancor. In view of our location so near the home of the immortal playwright, I was not surprised that the table talk turned to the subject of the theater. But the turn that the conversation presently took left me astonished. It was triggered by Dennis Romney.

Seated next to Holmes and smiling across the table at Mrs. Markham, Romney said, "It may come as a surprise to hear this, Mr. Holmes, but over the past few months, I have had the privilege of coaching Alice in the art of acting. I can state with confidence that you are dining in the presence of a future star of not only the Shakespearean stage, but a brilliant interpreter of the works of Mr. George Bernard Shaw and the drawing room dramas and comedy offerings of Mr. Oscar Wilde."

"That Mrs. Markham possesses the natural talents that are required in a great actress is not at all a surprise," Holmes answered. "She is playing a role at this moment and has been for quite some time."

With a quizzical expression, Romney replied, "You have the advantage of me, sir."

Peering intently at Mrs. Markham, Holmes said, "You can drop the pretense, madam. I know that you were once Mrs. Henry Dangerfield, and you know that I know."

She replied calmly, "You apparently are under the impression that I have kept my former identity a secret from my husband and Dennis. In fact, Geoffrey was in love with me before I met Henry Dangerfield. That is why Geoffrey stood by me during my trial on the false allegation that I was a murderess. Dennis also knows my unfortunate past, and he's been a darling to me "

With that remarkable statement, Geoffrey Markham shattered the forced civility between him, his wife, and the actor that had prevailed during the meal. Pounding the table so hard that he rattled the china and silver, he bolted up and was trembling as he shouted, "This is outrageous. I will not allow this humiliation to continue. Romney, I want you to get out."

Rising angrily, Romney replied, "I'll go only if Alice tells me to."

Deeply concerned about Markham's physical constitution after his immersion in the river and the possibly deleterious effect of his agitation on the state of health, I pleaded with him to retire immediately.

"Yes," said Holmes urgently. "For the sake of your well being, sir, you really must go upstairs and lie down."

Gesticulating wildly, he bellowed, "Mind your own business."

"Calm down, Geoffrey," appealed Mrs. Markham. "These gentlemen are correct. The best thing for you now is to go to bed. I assure you that you've worked yourself up over nothing We can sort all this out calmly in the morning. Take my hand and come along, I'll go up with you."

. As they withdrew, I said to Holmes and Romney, "I don't like her going with him. He's in such a state of jealous rage that he might lose all reason and do something terrible. He might even push her from the balcony and claim that she stumbled against that rotten railing and fell."

"Or it could happen the other way," said Holmes.

Romney blurted, "Sir, I demand you retract that calumny! Alice is not a murderess."

"We can't just stand by idly," I said urgently. "I think we'd better watch them from the doorway as they go up the stairs."

A moment later, my caution was justified. As we observed the balcony from below, I was horrified to see the pair in an apparent struggle close to the dangerously weakened railing. As we raced up the stairs, Mrs. Markham screamed, "He pushed me against the banister. He was trying to push me over."

"She's a liar," shouted Markham. "She attempted to do it to me."

"You may protest as much as you like, sir," said Holmes, "but it's you who's lying. And you might have gotten away with your scheme if I hadn't taken steps this afternoon to prevent your commission of a third murder."

"This is ridiculous," said Markham. "You will answer for this slander in the courts."

"I assure you, sir, that I shall welcome the opportunity to at last clear up the Dangerfield case in which the wrong person was in the dock. In the meantime, with the help of Dr. Watson and Mr. Romney, my first task is to see that you are securely trussed up pending the arrival of the local constabulary to arrest you for the attempt on the life of your wife, the murder of her uncle, and the arsenic poisoning of her first husband."

Within an hour, Markham was indeed taken away by the police with Holmes's pledge that he would provide the evidence required for a presentation of the case at the local assizes. All that remained was for him to explain his deductions and resulting actions to Mrs. Markham, Dennis Romney, and myself. He did so as we three sat by the parlor fireplace, sipping brandy as he stood before the hearth with a snifter in one hand and a pipe in the other. It was a pose that I had witnessed many times while he elucidated the solutions of numerous cases, most of which I later recounted for the benefit of history and some of which were so sensitive in their nature that he would not permit their publication.

"This afternoon while you all were away on your picnic," he began, "and having benefit of Watson's astute observations concerning the decayed balcony railing, as well as his fear that Mrs. Markham had the murder of her husband in mind, I took the precaution of entering this house in the company of the local carpenter to reinforce it. Of course, we know now that it was Mr. Markham who was planning to stage an accidental fall from the balcony."

"His purpose," I interjected, "was to collect on the life insurance policy he'd taken out on you, Mrs. Markham."

"Watson also deserves credit for that bit of information," Holmes continued. "Had he not mentioned it, I would not have turned my attention to Mr. Markham. But it was only when I was told by Mrs. Markham at dinner that he had been in love with her prior to her marriage to Henry Dangerfield that I was certain I'd been terribly wrong in the Dangerfield case. This left me with the suspicion that Markham had also killed the uncle. He hoped that by doing so he would marry into a sizeable inherited fortune. That plan went awry when the lady married someone else. With Dangerfield eliminated and the lady acquitted, he was free to marry her and eventually have not only the benefit of her inheritance, but the proceeds of an insurance policy upon her death."

"Am I correct, Holmes," I ventured, "in supposing that it was Markham who took the shot at you in the woods?"

"Exactly, my friend. He didn't want me on the scene when he staged his wife's death."

The terribly wronged woman gasped, "What kind of devil have I been living with?"

"I wish I could get my hands on that fiend," exclaimed Romney.

"That would make an exciting scene in a play, sir," Holmes said. "But Markham is in the proper setting now. British justice might occasionally be slow in coming, as it was in the Dangerfield case, but he will, I assure you get the ending he deserves. On the gallows."

· 4 ·

The Adventure of the
Blarney Stone

In my informal catalogue of various maxims pronounced by Sherlock Holmes in varying forms, the one that I noted most often was his rule that when you eliminate the impossible, what remains, however improbable, must be the truth. Second in frequency are statements regarding the necessity of never completely trusting the words or actions of a woman. Yet, in this man who formulated rules and laid down principles as if they were bricks in a wall, I frequently observed instances in which he disregarded his precepts and did the opposite. On one such occasion, when I called his attention to such a flouting, he explained with the strained patience of a father to a dense child, "The wonder of the workings of the mind is its capacity to accept two conflicting ideas and still be able to function."

Among contradictions that I observed in Sherlock Holmes during my years of association with the great man was his ability to abandon a tendency to stick close to home that bordered on aversion to leaving his beloved England to take up an investigation in another country. Records that I kept of his cases contain accounts of an astonishing number of adventures that began with a trip on the boat train from Waterloo Station to board the Channel ferry to Boulogne or Calais and from there to Paris or via the Orient Express to another city on the continent. On a few occasions, we took a steamer from Southampton to even more distant and exotic locales. Consequently, I was not surprised on a dreary afternoon in March of 1899 when he burst into our sitting room at 221B Baker Street with the demand, "Pack your bag, good fellow, we're leaving for Ireland at once."

"Where in Ireland?"

"The city of Cork."

I was keenly aware that Holmes was engaged at that time in pursuit of remnants of the gang that had operated at the direction of the late and unlamented Professor James Moriarty and his former associate Colonel Sebastian Moran, a scoundrel who had been subsequently nullified by being sent to prison for the murder of the Honorable Ronald Adair. Therefore, my assumption concerning a trip to Ireland was that he was following a surviving strand of Moriarty's complex web of malefactors to the Emerald Isle.

"It's murder, Watson," said Holmes as we packed for the journey to Liverpool and thence across the Irish Sea to Dublin and overland to our final destination on Ireland's southwest coast. "Do you believe in Leprechauns, also known to Irish folk as the "Little people?' "

"I have not believed in fairies and other such nonsense," I retorted, "since I was a child. Why do you ask?"

"According to brother Mycroft at the Home Office—"

"So that's where you've been all day."

"As I was saying, according to Mycroft, a series of murders committed in the city of Cork has become so entangled with Irish superstition and inflamed by the sensational press that the Irish Constabulary finds itself thwarted at every turn by those who do believe in Little People. We encountered the phenomenon in the person of the Widow McNamara in the adventure that you felt the need to dramatize under the title 'The Valley of Fear.' "

"I can't agree with you that I dramatized!"

"Simply noting the terrorist activities of the Scowrers and the daring and bravery shown by Birdy Edwards in infiltrating them would have been sufficient. Although he'd operated as a private detective, he was hewn from the same stone as other Irishmen who excel in police work in America. When I was in the United States, I could not fail to be impressed by the fact that the Irish make up a substantial proportion of the police forces in New York and Chicago. However, with the exceptions of Professor Moriarty and Colonel Moran, I have found the Irish curiously uninspired in the world of murder. England, Scotland, America, and Australia have all produced carefully and cleverly plotted homicides for greed or power, whereas murders in Ireland have been largely the result of uncontrollable passions."

Whether this rumination was a signal to me that Holmes had already deduced that the so-called Leprechaun murders that drew us to Ireland were rooted in dangerous emotion remains speculative. It was a case in which he elected not to explain to me how he concluded that the murderer was one Seamus Donnelly. When I pressed him on it, he responded with a dismissive gesture and asserted, "This matter is so insignificant that if you were to subject your readers to it, you would certainly jeopardize your literary reputation."

Because the departure of ships from Cork to England was delayed indefinitely by severe weather that brought a cold rain to the city, we found ourselves compelled to linger a few days in the charming port. Although Holmes never demonstrated the slightest interest in engaging in sight-seeing during our excursions into foreign lands, I welcomed the delay. I was interested in visiting one of the most famous sites in Ireland. A castle ruin in the nearby village of Blarney, a few miles from Cork, was renowned for a stone high in a wall that was purported to bestow upon anyone who kissed it the power of eloquence.

When I expressed my desire during dinner at our hotel in Cork to see the Blarney Stone, Holmes put down his fork and shook his head in dismay. "If you have a desire to dangle head-down some 100 feet above ground while someone holds tightly to your feet so you can kiss a slab of granite, or whatever the stone may be made of, you are free to do so," he said forcefully, "but you know very well my views on such superstitions. My policy is to keep my feet planted on the ground, even in Ireland."

"There would be no danger of my falling," I answered with a mischievous smile, "if you were the man holding onto my feet. And as you have so frequently noted regarding the quality of my writing, I appear to be in need of considerably more eloquence."

"Oh, very well! In the hope that there is something to this myth that will inspire you to pay more attention in your writings to my methods than to your romanticism, I'll accompany you to Blarney Castle in the morning. Weather permitting, of course."

To Holmes's obvious disappointment, the day proved sunny and warm. Our conveyance to the storied castle was a quaint

Irish jaunting cart on which we sat on the sides with our backs to each other. Why Erin is called the Emerald Isle was apparent in vistas of lush green pastures stretching before us in gently rolling waves. Our friendly driver, a rosy-cheeked fellow named Paddy Quinn, related in a charmingly lilting brogue how the tradition of kissing the Blarney Stone had originated. The legend states that in the mid-fifteenth century, a fellow named Cormack McCarthy, a descendant of the ancient kings of Munster and the builder of the castle, saved an old woman from drowning. In her gratitude, she promised him that if he climbed to the castle battlement and kissed a certain stone he would be rewarded with the gift of persuasive speech.

"From that day on," said the driver as Blarney Castle came into view, "himself became famous and powerful for his golden tongue, giving rise to the phrase 'talking the Blarney.' "

Reaching the stone required ascending several stories by way of a narrow stairway. As we emerged from the dim interior onto the glaringly sunlit battlement, we beheld not only the beauty of the Irish landscape, but a small cluster of men laughing heartily as one of them lay upon his belly clutching the ankles of another fellow who was dangling upside down in the crevice where the Blarney Stone was situated.

As the fellow was hauled out, his face was flushed and his hands were shaking. "Scariest thing I ever did," he exclaimed. "You'll never get me to do it again, no matter how drunk I am!"

With a chuckle as the men departed, Holmes patted my shoulder and said, "There seems to be no one else waiting to kiss the stone, old fellow. If you're still interested, I'll be pleased to lend you a hand. Both of them, actually."

That Holmes had the physical strength to hold me in position I had no doubt. Although he was seldom a man to take exercise for its own sake, he had demonstrated his fitness on many occasions. In the affair that I entitled "The Solitary Cyclist" he had proved not only stamina on a bicycle, but dexterity as a wheeler. I also witnessed him restore an iron poker to its original shape after it had been bent in half by the nefarious Grimesby Roylott. In the case of the Beryl Coronet he had boasted, "I am exceptionally strong in the fingers." During the adventure of the German spy Von Bork, he had asserted that he had a "grasp of iron."

What nettled me as we stood atop Blarney Castle was the same mocking tone that he'd adopted in an investigation of a hellish hound haunting Baskerville Hall, warning me with his tongue in cheek to avoid the moor, as he put it, "in those hours of darkness when the powers of evil are exalted." He had been similarly blatant in his disdain for superstition in the adventure of the Sussex Vampire.

"It will be interesting to learn," he continued in such a vein on the castle rooftop, "if a middle-aged, former army physician hanging head-down about one hundred feet from the ground in that narrow space between walls and kissing a slab of stone that's been caressed by lips of countless others gains the miraculous benefit promised."

Envisioning evenings seated fireside in Baker Street in which I would surely find myself subjected to teasing about my fascination with a legend that Holmes considered ludicrous, I said, rather defensively, "I never stated that I wanted to kiss the stone, only that I was keen to see the Blarney Castle."

"Well, now that you have, I propose that we find a respectable hotel in the town to stay the night and round out our excursion by partaking of some Irish cooking."

"An excellent idea! Tomorrow happens to be St. Patrick's Day. I expect that we'll find a festive atmosphere."

When we returned to our waiting jaunting cart and asked Mr. Quinn to recommend an inn and a place to eat in the town of Blarney, he indicated a public house in the only hotel. "The landlord is a friend of mine," he explained, "a lively fellow named Seamus Neary."

When we entered the pub, a gala scene greeted us. Green paper streamers hung from the ceiling, and green cloths draped the tables of scores of jovial diners. Happy-looking men stood shoulder to shoulder at a long bar, hoisting hefty mugs of dark beer or glasses of whiskey and exclaiming "Erin Go Bragh." While a burly waiter rendered "Sweet Molly Malone" in a fine tenor voice, a pretty red-haired barmaid showed us to a table at the rear of the room. When we were seated, she asked, "Will I be bringin' you a few drinks before your dinner, gentlemen?"

"Absolutely, my dear," said I. "What do you recommend?"

"There's nothing like a silky Irish whiskey to warm the cockles of your hearts and make you glow with a warm feeling so that the Little People will be apt to visit you."

"Whiskey it is or both of us."

"Yes, your honor," she replied with a charming little curtsey.

"I must say, Holmes," I ventured, raising my voice to be heard over the boisterous crowd as the girl withdrew, "I've never heard an English barmaid go into such rhapsodies over the virtues of a mere glass of whiskey. It's quite charming and endearing, isn't it?"

"In an earthy, peasant kind of way."

This rude remark reflected the contradictory nature of my friend which I have already noted. I often detected within him a streak of snobbery rooted in the English class system, which he could readily cast aside if a case required him to do so. His preferences when dining out were the elegance of Simpson's-in-the-Strand and the civility of Goldini's in the Gloucester Road or Marcini's prior to a concert at Covent Garden, yet he could appear quite at ease in the lowest pub in Whitechapel or amid the bustling crowd of the lunch counter at Charing Cross Station. While the social status of a client was irrelevant in taking on a case, and many who benefited from his assistance had little or no financial means, he always seemed more comfortable dealing with those who had wealth, although not for the sake of the money. He was always at pains to point out to a client that his fees were on an established scale that he never altered, except to remit them altogether.

As I ruminated upon Holmes's evident dismissal of the barmaid's behavior, we found ourselves accosted at our table by a clearly inebriated middle-aged man who blurted loudly, "You gentlemen are obviously English. I can't tell you what a relief it is to me to be among my own kind. Allow me to introduce myself. I am Jeffrey Hankin."

While I deemed Hankin's demeanor to be offensive in the extreme, Holmes greeted him cordially, invited him to sit with us and allowed him to pay for our drinks.

"I am a partner in the tweed mill that is this town's mainstay," Hankin said, "although you'd never know it from the disrespect these Irishmen show me when I visit the factory once a month, as compared to their attitude toward my Irish partner. He is seated over there and acting as though he's the cock of the roost just because he's Irish. His name is Michael Corcoran."

Observing that he was in the company of a beautiful woman, I asked, "Is that lady his wife?"

"No, sir, she's mine," Hankin replied. "Her name is Molly. She's Irish. Come along. I'll introduce you to both of them.

I'm sure they'll be thrilled to meet England's famous partners in crime detection."

"That's very kind," I replied, feeling embarrassed and awkward, "but I really don't—"

Holmes interjected, "We'd be delighted to meet them, sir."

Following the introductions, Mr. Corcoran asked, "What brings you gentlemen all the way to Blarney?"

Holmes replied, "Dr. Watson has always been interested in seeing Blarney Castle."

"Wonderful," said Mrs. Hankin. "Did you kiss the magical stone, Doctor?"

"I'm afraid I'm too old for such an athletic feat."

With a sour expression, Hankin said, "A lot of rubbish, if you ask me. Kissing a slab of stone! Utter nonsense!"

"But you must admit that it does require a good deal of courage."

"Fiddlesticks!"

"Is that why in all the years you've been coming to town to check up on how I'm running it that you haven't kissed the Blarney Stone, Jeffrey? No stomach for it?"

"Balderdash!"

"Balderdash is it? Well, how about proving you've got the mettle?"

"Mike, this is starting to get ridiculous."

"Maybe some money will make it seem less ridiculous. I'll wager ten pounds at ten to one odds that you haven't got what it takes."

With a glance at his wife, Hankin exclaimed, "You're on. But only on the condition that Mr. Holmes and Dr. Watson serve as witnesses, and to make sure you pay up when you lose! Is that agreeable, Mr. Holmes? Dr. Watson?"

"We'd be delighted to accommodate," said Holmes

"Very well," Corcoran asserted. "Shall we say at noon tomorrow?"

As the men shook hands, the singing waiter approached the table and proceeded to burst into another offering of "Sweet Molly Malone." "Good lord, not again," shouted Hankin. "I've heard enough of this caterwauling to last me a lifetime."

With that, he punched the waiter in the face with such force that he sent the young man reeling to the floor. Rushing to him, the barmaid asked, "Sean, are you all right?"

"Maybe now he'll think twice before blaring out with his stupid songs," said Hankin.

Rising angrily, the girl said, "I'll never be forgetting this, you drunken lout. And may the Little People lay a curse on you."

"Fiddlesticks," said Hankin as he staggered toward the door. "You can't frighten me with idiotic Irish superstitions."

Corcoran yelled, "Noon tomorrow, Jeffrey, or you pay me a hundred pounds!"

As Holmes and I returned to our table and the excitement subsided, I said, "Bless my soul, witnessing a barroom brawl on the eve of the day devoted to Ireland's patron saint was not at all what I'd expected. Our visit to Blarney has certainly proved interesting."

"It may be even more interesting tomorrow."

"What's happening tomorrow? Oh, you refer to the bet between Hankin and Corcoran."

"Precisely. My intuition tells that something is afoot, and I suspect that Mr. Hankin feels the same and is worried about it. If not, why should he make a condition of the bet that you and I be there when he kisses the Blarney Stone?"

"I find nothing more in this than an arrogant and exceedingly rude man who let drink and pride get the better of him."

"Your perennial problem, Watson, is that you see but don't observe."

"What I saw was a foolish fellow make a perhaps rash wager and take a poke at a waiter. Pray tell me, what I missed."

"There is obviously something going on between Hankin's wife and Corcoran. If you had been watching them after Hankin assaulted the waiter, instead of looking at the barmaid rushing to assist him, you would have observed that when Mrs. Hankin and Corcoran glanced at one another, they did so with a malice in their eyes directed toward Hankin that was more menacing than in the barmaid invoking a curse by the Little People. There are dark forces at work in this quaint slice of Ireland that rival those in any of the world's great cities."

"Or is it that you are finding menace in a commonplace situation simply because you feel bored? To cite the eminent Viennese psychoanalyst Sigmund Freud, I believe this is an instance in which a cigar probably is just a cigar."

"You and Dr. Freud may be right, my friend, but it is as dangerous for a detective to act or not act on the basis of probabilities as it is to operate on assumptions. Facts are what count. As to boredom, I admit that the rapid resolution of the Donnelly matter and the lengthy delay in returning to Baker Street and the excitement of London has left me with a sense of ennui. Which of us is correct we shall know at noon tomorrow."

"Isn't that an assumption on your part? How can you be sure that Hankin will keep the appointment with Corcoran, or vice versa?"

"Arrogance and pride! The former in the case of Hankin, because he's a typical example of too many Englishmen who believe Britain must rule the world, and the latter in Corcoran. He embodies the saying 'pride of the Irish.' It is those clashing attitudes that are at the root of the bloody history of the two peoples which began when the first Englishman set foot on Ireland and laid claim to it for the English Crown. I fear, Watson, that this conflict will carry on long after you and I no longer inhabit this mortal coil."

The day set aside by the Irish to honor Saint Patrick, and chosen by Corcoran and Hankin to settle their wager, dawned gloomy with the threat of rain. The only cheeriness I found was in the bright and smiling face of the pretty barmaid who served breakfast with the same winning way she had exhibited when describing the virtues of Irish whiskey. Her name, she said when I asked it, was Kathleen.

"After that fracas last night," she said as she brought us heaping plates of sausage and potatoes, "you gentlemen must be thinkin' poorly of us Irish folk But there was no call for that horrid man to punch Sean like that on account of his singin', and that's the truth. Then, to make the matter worse, that nasty creature added insult to injury by comin' around early this mornin' and offerin' Sean money to forget about what happened. The nerve of the man!"

At the appointed hour, Hankin appeared atop Blarney Castle to find Corcoran, Holmes, and I waiting. When Holmes noted that he was not accompanied by his wife, Hankin answered, "I'm afraid I'm in disgrace because of my behavior. Molly insisted that I see that waiter this morning and apologize."

"Did you?"

"Grovel before a waiter in front of that barmaid? Certainly not! I offered him money, but he rejected it. There's no explaining these Irish and their ways. Well, let's get this stupid farce over with before the rain comes so I can enjoy collecting the ten pounds from my partner."

A few moments later, Hankin sprawled at the edge of the damp parapet with Corcoran gripping his high boots at the ankles. But when Hankin maneuvered himself so that his body hung over the wall and Corcoran began lowering him, he shouted in horror, "I'm falling!"

Corcoran cried, "I'm trying to hold you, Jeffery. I'm trying!"

With that, Hankin's feet slipped from Corcoran's hands, and Hankin uttered a terrified scream as he plummeted a hundred feet to hit the ground with a sickening thud.

"I don't understand," Corcoran exclaimed as he rose. "I'm a strong man. He just slipped away from me!"

Rushing to Corcoran, Holmes seized his hands. Examining the palms, he said, "Grease! There's also a trace of boot blacking. This was no accident, sir. This was cold-blooded murder."

"Surely, Mr. Holmes," said Corcoran with a look of panic, "you can't think that I would do such a thing with you and Dr. Watson as witnesses."

"I make no such accusation, but it's obvious that someone knowing Hankin was going to kiss the Blarney Stone smeared his boots with grease, assuring that he would slip from the grasp of whoever was holding him. This is as clever a method of murder as ever I encountered."

As so often in the course of Sherlock Holmes's involvement in a criminal matter, either in the presence of a Scotland Yard official or a provincial constabulary, we found ourselves in the office of a Sergeant O'Malley as Holmes explained his theory of the crime. "Because of the changeability of the weather in this region, he said, "it's vital that the boots of the dead man be examined before it rains again."

"Don't concern yourself about that, Mr., Holmes," said O'Malley with an impish smile. "I know who it is I'll be arresting for this. I refer to Sean O'Flaherty."

Astonished by this assertion, I demanded, "On what basis can you suspect him?"

"The whole town of Blarney has heard about what happened in Neary's pub last night, an event which you and Mr. Holmes witnessed, I've been told."

"What is your evidence," demanded Holmes, "to charge O'Flaherty with murder?"

"The man had motive, did he not? And he had opportunity and the means. You see, Sean O'Flaherty is in charge of cleaning the boots at the hotel where Mr. Corcoran stays during his monthly visits to his factory. But there's no need for hurry in bringing in Sean. Seeing it's St. Patrick's Day, what would be the harm in letting him enjoy the last such celebration he will be having before they hang him? Once he's in custody, I'll see to the removal of the body and you and Dr. Watson can examine the dead man's boots to your hearts' content."

Although I was accustomed to feeling the blast of Holmes's dismay about the stupidity of local police officials and the bumbling of Scotland Yarders, particularly Inspector Lestrade, I'd never witnessed the fury he directed toward Sergeant O'Malley as we returned to the hotel. "In view of such rank malfeasance," he railed, "we are left with no alternative but to take this matter into our own hands, Watson. Starting with a call upon Sean O'Flaherty."

Having observed Holmes in action in such cases of police

incompetence, or to prevent a miscarriage of justice, including instances of letting suspects abscond, I worried that he intended to alert O'Flaherty of his impending arrest. Possibly because Holmes saw that I was brooding, he declared, "Set your mind at ease, old chap, I'm not contemplating commission of the felony of aiding and abetting an escape. I only wish to observe Sean O'Flaherty's reaction when I tell him of Hankin's murder, and that he is the only suspect."

"I see. If he bolts, he's admitting he's guilty."

"It is a capital mistake to theorize before you have all the facts."

For a man who may have committed murder, even if indirectly, O'Flaherty seemed to be as lighthearted as he was the previous evening. A large purple bruise and slight swelling of his jaw was evidence of his encounter with Hankin's fist as he sat at a small bench polishing boots. Looking up as we entered the room, he smiled and said, "Top of the morning to you, gentlemen. To what do I owe the honor of your visit on our blessed St. Patrick's Day?"

Picking up a brown riding boot, Holmes asked, "Did you know that the man who struck you last night is dead?"

"Jeffery Hankin's dead? Well, I can't think of anyone more deserving of sleeping under the sod. How did he die, may I ask?"

"He was murdered," said I.

"How was this happy deed done?"

Striving to contain my growing outrage at O'Flaherty's offensive tone, I responded, "He fell from the top of Blarney Castle when he was trying to kiss the stone."

"He fell because his partner, Mr. Corcoran, was unable to keep hold on his feet," Holmes interjected. "His boots had been greased."

"When you find the fellow who did the world the favor, I'd like to buy him a drink."

Holmes replied, "The police believe that because you clean Hankin's boots, you did it."

"I cleaned them this very morning, but I didn't put no grease on them."

"Are you aware that Kathleen the barmaid put the curse of the Little People on him after he knocked you down?"

"It's proud I am of her for it. Kathleen is a fine woman. She's to be my bride before the winter sets in."

At that moment, the young woman entered the room. "Ah, it's visitors, is it?" she asked blithely. "Good morning, gentlemen. How are you this fine day, Sean, my darlin'?"

"They've come to tell me that I'm soon to arrested for the murder of Jeffery Hankin. It seems that I greased his boots so he would fall from Blarney Castle."

With a silvery laugh, Kathleen shook her long red hair and said, "Greased boots was it? I can tell you who it was that greased them, gentlemen. It was the handiwork of the Little People because he insulted the Irish. You and everybody in the pub last night heard me call on them to work a curse on that wicked man for his spiteful tongue."

"Thank you both for your time," said Holmes excitedly. "You've been very helpful, and you can do so again by being at the gate to Blarney Castle at ten o'clock sharp."

"It was the Little People, sir," declared Kathleen as Holmes and I departed.

When we were out of earshot of the pair, I demanded "What's going on, Holmes?

"I believe I see it all now, Watson. But to prove what I suspect, we must pay another visit to the Blarney Castle. I want you to tell Sergeant O'Malley it is essential that he use the power of his office to see that Molly Hankin and Michael Corcoran are at the entrance to Blarney Castle at ten o'clock. In the meantime, I have some business to transact in the town."

Although I was brimming with curiosity as to his plan, I knew that at an appropriate time he would illuminate me. He had said to me on several occasions that I possessed the grand gift of silence and that this had made me quite invaluable as a companion. Consequently, when he left the hotel, he did so hearing no inquiries from me as to his purpose. When I told Sergeant O'Malley of Holmes's request, I found him surprisingly agreeable to employing his authority to assure the compliance of the late Mr. Hankin's widow and his former partner.

As we arrived precisely at ten and found the castle shrouded in mist, Kathleen and Sean were already there. Tipping his gray tweed deerstalker cap, he said, "In case no one told you, Dr. Watson, this weather is what we Irish call a soft day."

"Yes, and it's a dismal way to celebrate St. Patrick's day," grumbled Mrs. Hankin as she shifted a large handbag from one hand to the other in order to turn up her coat collar. "This dampness can get into your bones!"

"The weather is a little soggy," said the sergeant, "but I find all this fascinating."

A few moments later, Paddy Quinn's jaunting cart rattled to a stop in front of the gate and Holmes bounded out. "Excellent. Everyone's here. Thank you for your cooperation. Shall we go up? Careful how you go. Because of the dampness, the steps are probably slippery."

"Look here, Mr. Holmes," protested Corcoran as we went in, "what's this all about?"

"Oh dear, didn't Watson tell you? I intend to stage a re-enactment of the murder."

The caution about slippery steps proved embarrassingly correct. About halfway up the dim stairway, it was Holmes whose footing slipped, causing him to stumble against Mrs. Hankin. As we emerged, we saw that the inclement conditions on a special day for the Irish people, which ordinarily would have drawn numerous pilgrims to the legendary site, had resulted in the rooftop and battlement being unpopulated.

Striding to the opening in the parapet that provided access to the Blarney Stone and lying down, Holmes declared, "For the reconstruction of the crime, I'll assume the role of Mr. Hankin. Watson will grip my ankles in the same position taken by Mr. Corcoran. Ready, Watson?"

"Whenever you are, Holmes."

While we positioned ourselves, Sergeant O'Malley muttered, "Fascinating, indeed, but wholly unnecessary, since I already know who killed the man."

"If you mean me," exclaimed Sean O'Flaherty, "you're sadly mistaken."

With Holmes in place, I clasped his ankles and discovered to my horror that I could not maintain my grip. "Great scot, Holmes," I cried, "your boots are covered in grease!"

Bounding forward, Sergeant O'Malley grabbed the legs of Holmes's trousers. "Not to worry, old man," he shouted. "I've got a tight hold on you."

Reaching over the parapet, I grasped Holmes's coat tail and together with the sergeant pulled him up and onto the roof. As he dusted himself off, I exclaimed "That was a near thing."

"And a very illuminating thing, Watson. With your assistance,

I have demonstrated how the murder of Jeffery Hankin was committed."

"But we've know that all along," I said. "Hankin's boots had been greased so that Mr. Corcoran wouldn't be able to maintain his grip, just as I wasn't able to keep hold you."

"You have made my point, Watson. Unlike Mr. Corcoran, you immediately shouted out that grease had been applied to the boots, just as Mr. Corcoran would have to have noticed the grease on Hankin's boots the moment he touched them. The inescapable conclusion, therefore, is that the grease was on Corcoran's hands."

"I've heard enough of this," Corcoran objected vehemently. "Why should I want to kill my business partner?"

"You had two motives, sir, the second being your desire to get rid of your bothersome partner who felt the need to come to Blarney every month to check up on you. But your primary motivation was to be free to marry his wife. Don't insult me by trying to deny it."

Stepping forward, Molly Hankin declared, "You're wrong, Mr. Holmes. I'm the one that put the grease on Jeffery's boots. And I'm glad I did. This way, I saved all the Little People from having to do it."

"Thank you very much, Mrs. Hankin," said Holmes. "You have just proved that I am correct in observing that you and Michael Corcoran are in love. You've shown it by attempting to persuade me that he's wrongly accused. You do so in vain. I'm certain that I can prove that he is the guilty party once I'm able to examine Mr. Hankin's boots. If the grease had been applied by Sean O'Flaherty at the hotel, the grease would contain particles of dust that adhered to the grease while Hankin walked to the castle. I except to find none. That will prove that the grease was applied to the boots on this very spot."

"Until we examine those boots, Mr. Corcoran," said Sergeant O'Malley gravely, taking him by the arm, "I'm afraid you'll have to come along with me and spend St. Patrick's Day in official custody until a magistrate sorts all this out. But it doesn't look at all good for you."

Wrenching loose, Corcoran shouted, "Never. You'll not be locking me up. I'm terribly sorry, darling Molly. I do love you, but this Irishman is not for hanging."

Dashing to the parapet, he flung himself headlong over it.

Peering down, Sergeant O'Malley shook his head and said forlornly, "Now it will be two bodies I'll be having my men drag out of there come tomorrow."

"Tomorrow?" I objected. "Good Lord, man, you can't just leave them there."

"I appreciate how you feel, Dr. Watson, on account of you not being Irish, but there's no way I'd be able to muster enough eloquence to persuade the good men of this town to give up celebrating St. Patrick's Day, even if I were to kiss the Blarney Stone."

As we made our way down the castle steps, Sergeant O'Malley put into words a query that was also on my mind. "Holmes, you haven't explained how the grease got on your boots."

"Oh that. While Dr. Watson was arranging for you to bring Corcoran and the lady to the castle, I took some axle grease from Paddy Quinn's stable and then applied it to my boots when I pretended to slip and stumble on the stairs."

"Hanging from the wall of Blarney Castle with greasy boots was taking quite a chance."

"Not all. I knew I'd be held by Dr. Watson and that he

would detect the grease. Among his gifts, none of which he claims to have gotten from the Little People, is a sensitive touch."

· 5 ·

The Book of Tobit

An aspect of the activities of Sherlock Holmes that I have rarely noted in my published record of his numerous adventures and investigations was the necessity of his presence in courts to give testimony and present evidence in criminal cases. The result of frequent attendance at trials in London's Central Criminal Court, better known as the Old Bailey, was that he was as familiar a figure as the powdered-wigged and black-robed barristers and solicitors parading in its hallways and posturing in court chambers. I once noted in a list that I compiled of the strengths and the limits of his knowledge that he possessed a good practical knowledge of the law and respect for it. This may be why he was appalled that defense attorneys, most prosecutors, and many judges held the view that if a client were sufficiently illustrious, the rigid legal system should be elastic.

Along with this official involvement in trials, Holmes frequently exhibited an interest in Old Bailey proceedings with which he had no connection. Such was the sensational trial on the charge of murder brought against Major Edwin Beckwith. He stood accused of the stabbing death of his cousin, Sir Wilfred Vennering. It was alleged that he did so on the very night of the marriage of Sir Wilfred to one of the most fascinating and controversial women to attract the attention of Sherlock Holmes, ever since he undertook a commission from the hereditary king of Bohemia and found himself matching wits with the notorious adventuress Irene Adler.

Strikingly handsome even in widow's weeds, Lady Diana Vennering endured the trial with great poise and courage. As I observed her from the spectators' gallery on the first day of the trial, Holmes observed, "She has not only beauty in common with *the* woman, but both were in show business, if one can equate a career as a magician's assistant with one in the grand opera. Before marrying the magician her name was Jasmine LaFleur. Senor Rossoni was almost as good at the tricks and illusions of prestidigitation as the Great Harry Houdini, but without the panache or the worldwide fame."

"They divorced?"

"Really, Watson! Would Sir Wilfred Vennering jeopardize his exalted status in society by marrying a divorcee? No. The wedding to Senor Rossoni ended with his untimely death."

"Poor woman. Twice widowed!"

"The story becomes even stranger. Both men were murdered on their nuptial night."

"Great scot!"

"In the case of Rossoni, a painter who was LaFleur's unrequited suitor, named Peter Macombes, was briefly suspected,"

Holmes continued. "As to Major Beckwith, I believe there is a strong moral probability of guilt on the basis that he had become an embittered former suitor of the lady, but I have so far heard no evidence to support the case of the Crown against him."

As in so many sensational murder prosecutions that the Fleet Street newspapers seized upon to increase their circulation, the trial drew throngs of spectators, which were unabated from the first day to the last. As the jury retired to deliberate its verdict, the Metropolitan Police had to augment its force around and in the Old Bailey. After more than eight hours, jurors returned to validate Holmes's belief that the attorneys for the Crown had presented insufficient evidence for them to find Major Beckwith guilty.

Leaving the Old Bailey, Holmes and I discovered that the large crowd in the street did not agree with the verdict. One young man went so far as to loudly express his desire to hang the major himself. When this noxious outburst was greeted by the throng with cheers, he said that he would then direct his efforts to stringing up the jurors.

"What a disgusting and outrageous display," said I angrily. "So much for *vox populi.*"

"A jury of twelve men good and true is a sound system" Holmes replied. "As to the voice of the people, there are times when democracy seems to be the worst kind of government, except for all the others."

With the Beckwith murder trial concluded, the press moved on to other sensations in the interest of increased sales and Holmes found himself deeply enmeshed in the case of a document that went missing from the secret files of the Admiralty. While his brother Mycroft described the matter as of the utmost moment, with possible dire international consequences,

Holmes deduced that the paper had not been stolen, but was mistakenly placed in the wrong dossier.

On a dank and damp morning after the resolution of this matter, I returned to our Baker Street rooms after a brisk walk through Regent's Park in the hope of relieving a cramp in the leg, which was a reminder on such days that I had been severely wounded in the Battle of Maiwand in the Second Afghan War. I entered the sitting room to find Holmes perusing one of the city's more sensational newspapers. "Listen to this, Watson," he exclaimed. He read, " 'Emerging yesterday after two weeks in seclusion following the acquittal of Major Beckwith for the murder of her husband, Lady Vennering announced her intention to marry him before the year is out.' "

"What a bizarre development."

"How many times have you heard me say that life is infinitely stranger than fiction?"

"Innumerable!"

"This proves again what I have often said, that love is inexplicable."

"I knew from what came out in the trial that Beckwith was in love with Lady Vennering, but I had no inkling that she reciprocated."

"I also failed to recognize it. Of course, the fair sex has always been your department."

"There is an American saying, to wit, the third time is a charm. Perhaps that will prove true for Lady Vennering's third marriage and the woman will at last he spared the attention of the scandal-seeking newspapers."

"Members of the press are cats and women of that sort are catnip."

During the ensuing weeks, Sunday editions of the newspapers

devoted extensive space to Lady Vennering. They delved into the details of her life as a performer in a magic act, her two tragically brief marriages, regurgitations of the trial of Beckwith and plans of the forthcoming wedding. While reading one of these articles, I observed Holmes at the window overlooking Baker Street with an expression that conveyed more than idle curiosity. "What is it now," I asked, "that you find so compelling in the passing parade?"

Turning away from the window, he said, "I believe we are about to have a visitor. He is a clergyman, young and extremely agitated. He's been walking up and down for ten minutes and looking up at our window. I haven't decided if feels as though he is a martyr about to be burned at the stake, or an inquisitor preparing to light the faggots. Ah! He's crossing the street. We'll know what's troubling him in a few moments."

Handsome and slender, he introduced himself as the Reverend Arthur Whelan. Invited to take a chair, he began pacing nervously as he stated, "This is a very difficult subject to broach, Mr. Holmes. It's only after intense personal conflict that I've been able to come to you. Are you familiar with the Book of Tobit in the Holy Bible?"

"The Book of Tobit?" I said. "I've never heard of it."

"You won't find it in your copy of the King James Authorized Version," said Holmes. "The Book of Tobit is in a collection of noncanonical Old Testament writings known as the Apocrypha. The story relates how a devout Jew in exile in Assyria by the name of Tobit and his son Tobias were rewarded for their piety and good deeds. Despite this, Tobit was blinded. As he prayed for God to end his life, a widow named Sarah also beseeched the Almighty for death because each of her seven husbands was killed by a demon by the name of Asmodeus on their wedding night."

"You know your Bible, sir," said the clergyman.

"What is your connection with Lady Vennering?"

"I'm a friend."

"And clearly a worried one. Why?"

"I'm troubled by something that did not come out in the trial of Major Beckwith, which now, in view of the announced betrothal, causes me great concern."

"If you had evidence," said I, "why didn't you present it?"

"Diana, that is Lady Vennering, asked me not to come forward. But now I can no longer remain mute."

"You've done the right thing," I said, "in confiding in Holmes."

"Tell us what you were asked not to reveal," Holmes demanded, "why Lady Vennering was so insistent, and why she has changed her mind."

Ceasing his pacing, Whelan answered, "Before each of Lady Vennering's husbands was killed, they received a note warning that if they married her, they would be murdered."

"Have you seen these notes?"

"I've seen the one received by Sir Wilfred. Lady Vennering showed it to me yesterday. It said that if the wedding proceeded, his hours were numbered. It was signed Asmodeus."

"What do wish me to do, sir?"

"I want you to speak to her and urge her not to go through with marrying Beckwith."

"Why do you suppose she would agree to see me?"

"She will, if only to humor me. You see, I did an un-Christian thing. In another context, you might call it blackmail. She's a member of my flock. As such, I performed the ceremony at both her weddings. I told her that if she didn't see you, I would not officiate again."

"Where does she reside?"

"She inherited Sir Wilfred's house in Berkeley Square. I took the liberty of telling her that you would call on her this afternoon. Will you, Mr. Holmes?"

"As it happens, I have no pressing business at the moment."

As the Reverend Mr. Whelan made his way down the stairs, I was astonished to find Holmes laughing. Finding this odd, I asked, "Is it amusing that I did not know of the Book of Tobit?"

"The joke, dear fellow, is that the role of protector that I've been given by our visitor was undertaken in the Book of Tobit by the Archangel Raphael. Do I bear any resemblance whatever to an instrument of God?"

Although Holmes had a rich knowledge in many diverse subjects and was never reticent to give his opinion on them, I had not observed an interest in religion and recalled that he had spoken to me about a Divine Power but once. The occasion was prompted by his observation of a flower. He had been investigating a case in which a civil servant named Percy Phelps came under suspicion concerning the disappearance of a secret naval treaty he had been copying. As Homes contemplated a wilting stalk of moss rose by an open window, he said quietly, "There is nothing in which deduction is so necessary as in religion. Our highest assurance of the goodness of Providence seems to me to rest in the flowers. It is only goodness which gives extras, and so I say that we have much to hope from this single rose."

On the way to our meeting with Lady Vennering, Holmes asked, "What do you make of the story related by the Reverend Mr. Whelan?"

"He may be a man of the cloth, but I sensed that he regards Lady Vennering as more than a member of his congregation. I suspect that he's in love with her."

"Do you also suspect that he's so enamored that he could be responsible for the deaths of her husbands?"

"The idea has crossed my mind. He knows the story in the Book of Tobit and may have written the threatening notes in order to frighten Rossoni and Vennering out of going through with the marriages. Wearing a clerical collar does not exempt a man from committing the sin forbidden by the commandment that thou shalt not kill, or any of the other nine."

"Indeed. However, murderous clergy have not been nearly as abundant as physicians who bore the mark of Cain."

As our hansom drew to a halt in front of the Berkeley Square mansion, I found myself increasingly nervous at the prospect of meeting the woman who had become the talk of London through no fault of her own. I had watched her at the Beckwith trial from a distance and admired her fortitude and composure as she gave testimony concerning the deaths of her two husbands. Greeted by her in the graciously appointed parlor of the large house, I felt my anxiety melt away. Her beauty was exceeded only by her charming demeanor.

"I'm delighted to meet you, Mr. Holmes, and you, too, Dr. Watson," she said as tea was served, "but I'm afraid Arthur has imposed on you unnecessarily. He's a dear friend, but he does have a way of exaggerating things."

"Would it be possible for me to examine the threatening note that Sir Wilfred received?"

"I'm sorry. When I showed it to Arthur yesterday, he was so upset that I burned it."

"Why did you want the existence of it and the one to sent to your first husband kept out of the record of the trial?"

"I was afraid that the prosecution would accuse Major Beckwith of sending them."

"Where is your fiancé at the moment?"

"He's probably at his club, but I must ask you not to involve him in this matter. He has been through enough already."

"As you wish, madam. Should you desire my assistance, I'm at your disposal."

"You are very kind. Thank you. But I'm sure that will not be necessary."

Pausing at the door, Holmes asked, "When do you and Major Beckwith plan to marry?"

"We haven't settled on a date. Soon. It will be a quiet ceremony. To avoid the press, it will not be announced until after Edwin and I have left on our honeymoon."

"Where will you be going?"

"We plan to spend our wedding night at the Savoy Hotel and depart in the morning for Southampton to sail to America. We'll be away a month."

"I'm sure Dr. Watson joins me in wishing you both happiness."

"Indeed I do, Lady Vennering," said I most heartily.

"Fascinating woman," Holmes declared as he hailed a cab. "I haven't met her like since the Bohemian affair. Are you hungry? What say you to an early dinner?"

"A capital idea. Where do you suggest?"

"I was thinking of Simpson's in the Strand, but first, what about a drink or two to whet our appetites, say at the Savoy?"

"I see what you're up to, Holmes. I know your methods. You have spies everywhere! Who is it at the Savoy that you intend to engage to inform you immediately of the presence at the hotel of the newlyweds?"

"Watson, you are a marvel! His name is Claiborne. He is the head concierge."

Having made the arrangement to be promptly informed when

the couple arrived, Holmes said nothing more of Lady Vennering and plunged into investigating a case involving a client of the lower class whose only familiarity with hotels such as the Savoy was gained by reading about it in the society notices in newspapers. It was a complex case, which absorbed Holmes for more than two weeks. On the evening he returned to Baker Street to report its successful conclusion with the arrest of the unfortunate fellow's brother, Holmes and I had just settled down to one of Mrs. Hudson's plain but satisfying dinners, only to be interrupted by a messenger in the uniform of the Savoy Hotel.

"Mr. Claiborne says that you must come at once, sir," the boy exclaimed. "There's been an awful murder."

Upon our arrival, we were greeted by Inspector Lestrade. He demanded, "How did you find out about this so fast, Holmes? The body wasn't discovered but an hour ago."

"How was Major Beckwith killed?"

"Blimey! Who told you it was him? He was stabbed in the back in the bath."

"Who found him?"

"His wife. She's the former Lady Vennering. They were just married. Sound familiar?"

"Have you settled on a suspect?"

"There are two possibilities. One is a painter by the name of Peter Macombes. He did a portrait of Lady Vennering, and from what I've heard, he fell madly in love with her. The other is the Reverend Mr. Arthur Whelan, also rumored to be smitten with her. What's your interest in all this, may I ask?"

"Murder is my business. I'd appreciate being kept informed of developments."

Despite this assertion, Holmes seemed to me to immediately lose all his interest in the matter. On occasions when I called his attention to an article on the case in the press, he showed the utmost indifference. At last, in frustration and out of curiosity, I boldly ventured, "I find your indifference regarding the Beckwith murder mystifying."

"When my services are proffered and rejected out of hand," he retorted, "that is the end of the matter."

Nor was he the least stimulated a month after the murder when Lestrade inevitably came plodding up our stairs to admit he had made no headway toward solving it. Ordinarily, Holmes savored such a moment. Instead, he turned upon Lestrade and exclaimed, "Although you assume that I am constantly at the disposal of Scotland Yard to supply its deficiencies, I am not!"

This outburst was especially puzzling not only because Holmes was not then engaged in an investigation, but had been complaining about his inactivity that very day, declaring, "What's become of the criminals, Watson? Where are the great crimes? Has the devil gone on holiday?"

My concern regarding his morose disposition raised a fear that I believed had been laid to rest. I was afraid that if he were not presented a problem to solve, he might return to his use of cocaine. To my utter astonishment and his, three days after Inspector Lestrade was sent packing, the gloomy atmosphere of 221B Baker Street was suddenly dispelled by the delivery of a note from Lady Vennering.

"Ah ha," said Holmes exultingly, "she wishes to see me."

The gracefully penned note read:

Dear Mr. Holmes,

I wish to thank you, perhaps unforgivably belatedly, for the kindness and concern that you expressed when you called upon me. Now that time has passed since the tragedy of Major Beckwith's death, I hope that you will call on me again so that I may tender my regrets in person.

Diana

Thus began an extraordinary sequence of events that left me astounded and bewildered. Holmes began behaving in a manner that I had never witnessed in all our years of association. Suddenly, he was rarely at home in the evenings. He preferred to attend the theater or the opera with Lady Vennering. Cases that should have interested him were rejected. Clients promising enormous retainers were brushed aside. Even Mrs. Hudson expressed amazement.

"If I didn't know Mr. Holmes as well as I do, and his distrustful attitude toward women," she said with a chuckle, "I'd think that he's fallen in love."

"Love? My good woman, he is indelibly on record on that subject. He believes that all emotions, and that one in particular, interfere with his thought processes."

After several weeks of Holmes's uncharacteristic behavior, perhaps because of medical training as much out of friendship, I decided to confront him with the same bluntness with which I had protested his indulgence in opiates. While he was dressing to go to the theater, I declared, "Look here Holmes, we've been friends for a good many years now—"

"Quite so."

"Therefore, I feel I'm entitled to speak to you straight from the shoulder."

"Of course you are."

"Very well. This Diana Beckwith is making a fool of you. You gad about as if you were a fellow of twenty. What's come over you?"

"Perhaps you'd better fortify yourself with a brandy, my friend. Diana and I are getting married. The ceremony is tomorrow. It's short notice, but I hope you will be my best man."

"This is insane! Have you forgotten that three of this woman's husbands were murdered on their wedding night?"

"I assure you, old friend, that in this instance no man will succeed in putting asunder the man and woman whom God has joined together, and neither shall anyone named Asmodeus."

"Who will be presiding at the ceremony? The Reverend Mr. Whelan?"

"He has again refused. My brother Mycroft has recommended a Nonconformist minister by the name of Vernet."

"Mycroft has given his blessing to this marriage?"

"He was quite enthusiastic, but pressing matters at the Foreign Office will prevent him from attending."

This was not the first time Holmes had informed me that he had become engaged. In the case of the blackmailer Milverton, he had promised marriage to the housemaid. It was a ruse to gain entry to Milverton's house and burglarize it. The pledge of marriage was given with confidence that a rival for the maid's hand would cut him out, which is what happened. Explaining using the girl in such a deceitful way, he noted, "You must play your cards as best you can when such a stake is on the table."

Accompanying Holmes to the church the following afternoon, I gazed at Holmes's happy countenance and shed my misgivings. Less than an hour later, the Reverend Mr. Vernet pronounced Holmes and the thrice-widowed bride man and wife. A small reception was laid on at the Savoy. To my surprise, considering Holmes's last encounter with Lestrade, I found the inspector there and learned that he remained stymied in his search for the killer of Major Beckwith. Presently, bride and groom retired to the Bridal Suite, insisting as they went that the reception continue.

Half an hour later as Lestrade and I were sipping champagne, Holmes burst into the room and exclaimed, "You may make the arrest now, Lestrade. The triple murderer is tied up in the Bridal Suite! Come along, Watson, and allow me to introduce you to Asmodeus. Oh yes, I forgot to tell you that I received one of the threatening missives this morning."

When Holmes opened the door to the Bridal Suite, the woman he had just married was trussed up in a chair. "The knife she intended to use to kill me is on the bureau," said Holmes. "Fortunately for me, it has a mirror that allowed me to observe her draw the knife, as I knew she would eventually."

"Good work, Mr. Holmes," said Lestrade.

"This was all a plan, Holmes," said I. "You knew she was a murderess all along! How?"

"When Lestrade informed me that his investigation proved that none of his suspects could have murdered Major Beckwith, the only possible explanation was that he was killed by his bride. At that point, it was vital that she believe Scotland Yard's investigation was at a dead end. To be certain of this, Diana sought confirmation from me, hence her invitation to me. This provided me the occasion to tell her that Inspector Lestrade had come to me for assistance, but that I had kicked him out."

"That was also a charade?"

"I had to be certain that if she had the occasion to ask you about my refusing to assist the police, you would attest to it."

"What was the woman's motive in killing her husbands?"

"I never guess. The motive is for Lestrade to ultimately determine. I do have a suspicion, however, that the lady realized she had better pickings in Sir Wilfred than in the magician.

She planned to kill Vennering for the inheritance. When she learned about the Book of Tobit from the Reverend Mr. Whelan, she wrote the Asmodeus note to him and then destroyed it. That's why the only note she had to show Whelan was the one she inflicted on Major Beckwith."

"Why did she marry him?"

"To lend credibility to the Asmodeus trick. It was a sleight of hand worthy of her first husband. And victim."

"This is all well and good, Holmes. But you are still married to her. Under British law, you can't be a witness against her."

"If you had taken a closer look at the clergyman who performed the marriage ceremony," Holmes replied, "you might have discerned that beneath the gray mutton whiskers and the thick lenses of his spectacles was my remarkably versatile brother. When I broached the subject of his playing the role, Mycroft jumped at the opportunity to finally don the regalia of a man of the cloth, if only for a short time."

"What do you mean by *finally* don the regalia?"

"For a mercifully brief period in his youth, Mycroft's mind was quite set upon entering the clergy. Fortunately, for various Prime Ministers, Her Majesty's government in Whitehall, the Parliament, and myself, he came to the realization that he was far better suited for intrigues of politics and international affairs than for those of the Church of England."

With a chuckle, I said, "I do find it difficult to picture Mycroft presiding over baptisms and other responsibilities of the clergy."

"Although I'm gratified that Mycroft chose another path in life," said Holmes as he lit a pipe, "I find myself wondering from time to time what it would be like to be the brother of the Archbishop of Canterbury. I have no doubt that Mycroft would one day have ascended to that lofty and venerable position. You also should have suspected that something was afoot in the wedding ceremony when you heard the name of the person who performed it."

"Vernet. What about it?"

"If you will review your account of the case of the Greek interpreter, you will find that I informed you that my grandmother was the sister of the French painter of martial pieces by the name of Emile Jean Horace Vernet."

"Now I remember. You said, 'Art in the blood is liable to take the strangest forms.' "

"The same applies to crime, Watson. If it didn't, I would be unemployed."

·6·

The Haunting of Sherlock Holmes

In October of 1899, Sherlock Holmes and I undertook a European journey that led us into a tangle of political intrigues in a minor Balkan kingdom. We encountered revolutionary ferment, espionage, a romance between a prince and a young woman who sang for her supper, and a voice speaking from beyond the grave. This singular odyssey began with Holmes returning from a visit to his tobacconist in Whitehall Place and announcing that he was yielding to my pleas that he take a holiday. The previous ten months were one of the most challenging periods in the career of the world's first and most renowned private consulting detective.

The year had commenced with the unpleasant business of Charles Augustus Milverton, an affair that I described as an absolutely unique experience. May brought the disappearance of the famous Black Pearl of the Borgias and Holmes's disappointment that he was not called upon by Scotland Yard for assistance. I am certain that had he been consulted promptly, a sinister case involving murder, revenge, and a series of thefts of cheap plaster busts of Napoleon would not have remained unresolved for more than eight months. Between bringing to a finish the evil reign of the repulsive blackmailer and his intervention in the matter of the Borgia pearl, he unmasked the Cook-Singleton forgery, solved the kidnapping of Count Ivo Bogdanovic in broad daylight in Regency Street, the case of the Camden Town Strangler, and two episodes that were of no importance to anyone except those directly affected.

"Finding myself unengaged," said Holmes, "I have decided that now is a propitious time to take that holiday you've been insisting upon." Laying down a large bundle that I assumed was an abundant supply of his preferred small, black, and malodorous Sumatran cigars and several tins of strongly aromatic pipe tobacco that smelled like burning rope, he continued, "Did I ever tell you that I have always had a desire to swim in the Black Sea?"

"In all the years of our association, Holmes, you have never expressed a desire to dip a toe in any body of water except a bathtub."

"I was quite good at aquatics in my youth. I placed first twice in freestyle races while at Oxford. Now I swim in the murky waters of crime. As to our holiday, I thought we might take the Orient Express to Belgrade and wend our way through the Balkans to the tiny principality of Kazanlak and its capital, Groznia, on the Black Sea coast. I'm told that it's particularly charming and that the weather in October is perfect. I am also informed that most of the locals are fluent in English. This is due primarily to the influence on the present monarch, Prince Alexei, of my elder brother Mycroft. He was the prince's tutor at Cambridge after Alexei was forced into exile in England during one of the periodic upheavals that are a feature of Balkan politics."

"Is there *anyone* of prominence that your brother doesn't know?"

"There is one such person. Mycroft has yet to meet the young up and coming American politician Theodore Roosevelt, whose friendship I enjoyed when I was in New York City in the summer of 1880. We assisted Wilson Hargreave of the New York Police Bureau in investigating a murder with political ramifications. Roosevelt later served as the Police Commissioner. At the moment, TR, as he prefers to be addressed, is the governor of New York State. He was elected following his return from seeing action in the Spanish-American War. As the leader of a cavalry regiment bearing the name 'Rough Riders,' he was quite heroic in leading a charge up a vital hillside. In my opinion, with which Mycroft agrees, Roosevelt will soon be president of the United States. As such, Mycroft expects him to project American power in the affairs of a world in which Mycroft has been a potent, although behind-the-scenes, manipulator."

"This is all very interesting, but it's off the point. When do you plan to leave for your holiday in the Balkans?"

"Our holiday, Watson! You're coming with me. I stopped at the Orient Express offices and booked us for Monday."

"I have a mere two days to prepare?"

"Because we'll be away for three weeks," he said as he opened the bundle, "I purchased more than my usual number of cigars and tobacco tins, so there's no danger of our running short."

During the crossing to Calais and aboard the famous

cross-continent train, I could not dislodge from my thoughts the memory of a similar trip almost ten years before when Holmes left London in the shadow of a death threat from Professor Moriarty, only to encounter him with a deadly result for the evil genius at the Reichenbach Falls in Switzerland. During that journey, Holmes warned me that he had become a dangerous traveling companion. No such concern was present as we ventured serenely toward a Black Sea town in a land of which I had never heard, but about which Holmes either knew a great deal, or had learned in anticipation of our trip.

"The Balkans are a fascinating problem," he said with the same enthusiasm he exhibited at the start of a promising investigation. "With people of different religions—Roman Catholics, Eastern Orthodox, Jews, and Muslims—and a bitter shared history, they are a breeding ground for trouble. Steeped in the rivalries of the great European powers to the west and of Russia on the east, the Balkans are a powder keg that may one day explode and set the entire world aflame."

"Careful, Holmes. You're starting to sound like Mycroft. We're on holiday, remember?"

"And a better companion a man could not have!"

When we arrived in Groznia, the capital of the principality of Kazanlak proved to be the picturesque setting Holmes had promised. Overlooking the placid waters of the Black Sea, it curled against western mountains in warming sunlight. Among the amenities of the quaint town was a stately opera house. In this idyllic setting and relaxing atmosphere, I hoped that Holmes would find respite from a physically strenuous and emotionally draining year and would embrace the peace and quiet of anonymity. Our hotel, Holmes informed me as if he were a tour guide, had been converted from a castle that legend said had been a resting place for Crusaders to and from the Holy Land. Off the cavernous lobby was a restaurant that in the evenings offered the music of a small orchestra and both folk songs and operatic arias by a beautiful young Hungarian soprano, by the name of Lily Rainer, who was touring European capitals.

After a splendid meal on the very first evening as I was enjoying her truly delightful and accomplished performance, Holmes whispered, "The young man in the magnificent uniform who is accompanied by quite an entourage of bodyguards is Crown Prince Stefano. He is heir to the throne. He studied in America. His younger brother, Rudolfo, is a colonel and a martinet who was schooled in Prussia. Their younger sister, the Princess Royal Alexandra, is the best of the lot. Judging by the fact that Stefano hasn't taken his eyes off Miss Rainer since she took to the stage, I venture that the young man's fascination with in her is not entirely motivated by her vocal virtuosity. He shows all the signs of a man who has fallen hopelessly in love."

"If that is the case, it is truly hopeless," I replied. "Miss Rainer is not only a commoner, but a foreigner. Marriage is out of the question."

At that moment, we were accosted—and that is the proper word—by the commissioner of police. With beady black eyes set deeply in a sallow, thin ratlike face, Paolo Krasznadar struck me as a Balkan version of Inspector Lestrade. He spoke English with a thick accent that required close attention to fathom, but left no doubt that he was a policeman as he pulled up a chair and asked, "May I inquire what attracts the well-known Sherlock Holmes and his also illustrious biographer to our fair but humble city? Are you on the trail of an international jewel thief? A banker who absconded with all the money? Is it a *femme fatale,* perhaps, of the caliber of Miss Irene Adler? I am familiar with that notorious adventuress because my wife is a former actress and knew Miss Adler professionally in Vienna."

"My purpose is leisure, sir," Holmes answered.

"In any case, I bid you welcome. Still, it is disappointing to a lowly local police official. I allowed myself to imagine the honor of assisting you."

As Miss Rainer finished rendering a lively folk tune to enthusiastic applause from the prince, a small audience of Groznians and an elderly couple who looked German, I asked the commissioner, "Have you a problem with crime in your city, sir?"

"What city doesn't?" he replied with a Lestrade-like smirk. "Our miscreants and felons find that Kazanlakian justice is swift and very often final. Nothing deters crime as effectively as the imposition of severe penalties, don't you agree?"

"In England we also believe in tempering justice with mercy."

"That is an indulgence, Dr. Watson, that is available to a very few nations that have had a long history and a settled system of politics in which changes in government are by means of ballots, not bullets. It's not the case in this region of the world, and certainly not in Kazanlak."

"Are you telling us that Prince Sergei's throne is imperiled?"

"There are elements within the country who have support from without and agitate for an end to monarchy," he said with a glance at the German couple, "but I have my eyes on them."

When the commissioner of police at last bade us goodnight with a wish that Holmes and I would enjoy our holiday, I said, "This is a fine place that you've picked for a vacation, Holmes. From what that policeman says, we may be in the middle of a revolution at any minute."

"Not tonight, I hope. I'm having a very good time. This singer was quite enchanting and remarkably versatile. One minute, she rendered Puccini and the next, a saucy English music hall ditty. She has quite a cosmopolitan repertoire. As to the chief of the constabulary, I could not help observing that you don't care for him."

"Damned intrusive of him, helping himself to a chair and sticking his nose into why you are here. It's none of his business."

"He has the natural curiosity of the policeman, Watson. He would be a rare one indeed if Sherlock Holmes appeared in his domain and he did not wonder why. How better to find out than by offering us welcome?"

"You may believe the man had nothing more in mind than bidding us welcome, but I say he's up to something."

"What a suspicious character you've become, Watson."

"I was merely applying one of your precepts, that when one fact points in one direction, if you shift your own point of view a little, you may find it pointing to something different."

"Well done! Whether I am right or you, only time will tell."

The next morning as we toured the ancient town, I informed Holmes that I was certain we were being followed.

"Since we left the hotel," Holmes replied. "There are three watchers, switching every fifteen minutes. It's been very amusing. This trio could certainly profit by spending a day with Wiggins and the Baker Street irregulars. Such amateurish behavior means they are not police. Whoever they are, the least we can do is make their day worthwhile in terms of exercise."

Accordingly, we gave them a workout by tramping for hours and many miles before we returned to the hotel half an hour before dinner. As we entered the restaurant, we were greeted by

Commissioner Krasznadar and found ourselves invited to dine with the young heir to the Kazanlak throne.

"This is indeed an honor, sir," said I with an appropriate bow.

"Quite so," said Holmes as we sat at a table directly in front of the platform where Miss Rainer would be singing. "Was it your men who accompanied Dr. Watson and me during our walk around Groznia today?"

Through a flicker of a smile found on the faces of boys who have been caught with their hands in the cookie jar, the prince exclaimed, "I don't know what you mean."

"One of the three men resembled a member of your retinue last night, but obviously I'm mistaken. It's of no moment."

"Hardly, sir," objected Krasznadar. "If you and Dr. Watson were followed, it is a matter of the utmost moment to me as commissioner of police."

With a mischievously boyish grin, Prince Stefano interjected, "You must be patient with Paolo, Mr. Holmes. Every night he looks under his bed for a spy or revolutionary."

The policeman's expression turned grim. "You may make a joke about such things, Your Highness, but the attention I have devoted to finding persons who seek to overthrow your father has resulted in what I'm afraid will come as a terrible blow to you. It is my duty to inform you, sir, that this evening I intend to arrest Lily Rainer on the charges of espionage and complicity in a revolutionary conspiracy against the government of Kazanlak."

With flushed face, the prince leapt to his feet. "Preposterous!"

"The evidence is incontrovertible. She was observed after her performance last evening passing documents of a sensitive nature to a German couple who are now in custody and will be executed by firing squad at dawn. They also had in their possession several letters given to them by Lily Rainer from the leader of the revolutionists, a person known only as Josef."

"This is outrageous," said I. "How can you execute people without a trial?"

"There was no need for a tribunal. They confessed. I expect Miss Rainer to do so. When she does, she will reap the same fate as the pair arrested last night. Unfortunately, Germany has been providing assistance to revolutionaries in Kazanlak, with the aid of Lily Rainer, who as an international celebrity was able to travel here freely. I've had my eyes on her a long time."

A grim silence kept by the crown prince ended with a pained sigh. "I find this hard to believe! I must see the evidence, Commissioner," he declared. "If it is as you have stated, then I, Prince Stefano Wilhelm Yosephus Constantine, will personally command the firing squad!"

Despite a suggestion by Holmes that the prince attempt to persuade Lily Rainer to provide information on the conspiracy and lead the police to the mysterious Josef and a remonstrance of Commissioner Krasznadar that he was engaging in a rush to judgment, the execution was held at dawn with the prince giving the order to fire. Unable to sleep in our room in the converted castle close to the courtyard of the Ministry of Justice, we heard the rifle volley that claimed her life.

After a long, pensive moment, I stirred from my combined sadness at what had happened and outrage over a woman having been executed and said to Holmes, "It seems duty to one's country has overcome love. Unless, of course, you were mistaken in deducing that the prince was enamored of the woman."

"I admit that I am not the expert in affairs of the heart that you have proven yourself to be on so many occasions, my sentimental friend, but I stand by my observation."

Resigned to the tragedy, we agreed that our Balkan holiday was over and that we would depart Groznia as soon as possible. As we went to the door to go down for what we hoped would be our last breakfast in that country Holmes bent down and said, "Hello, what's this? It appears that a note has been slipped under the door. Addressed to me. Printed words. A woman's hand. Small envelope. Quality paper. The watermark is a London firm."

The note was also in printed letters.

It read:

My Dear Mr. Holmes,

I swear to you that I am wrongly accused. You could not save my life, but only you can restore my honor and that of my family by proving I was not a spy and revolutionary. Consider this a voice calling for justice from beyond the grave.

Lily Rainer

"This is a first, Watson. Our agency has always scoffed at intimations of the supernatural, yet we find ourselves with a ghost for a client!"

"Surely, you don't intend to do what the note requests? The woman is dead and buried, and the political affairs of this misbegotten country are not our concern. Krasznadar obviously had sufficient evidence to convince the prince of Rainer's guilt."

"If she was guilty, why should she send me a note? An even

more interesting question is how she managed to do so from prison. These are deep waters, Watson. I have no choice but to follow through. However, I make you this promise. After two days, if I am satisfied that I have been wasting time on a wild ghost chase, so to speak, we pack up and leave on the next train."

"Very well. Two days."

"Good man!"

"How may I be of assistance?"

"Because we are being watched on someone's orders, I want you to make it known to the hotel staff that I have taken ill and must not be disturbed. Meanwhile, I shall slip out and take the measure of this place in terms of whether this revolutionary threat that the commissioner believes is real has any popular support."

"You're a foreigner. You'll stick out like a sore thumb."

"After I shake off anyone who might be following me, I will make a surreptitious visit to the opera house. I intend to help myself to a bit of makeup and borrow a few articles from the costume department."

Following a hearty breakfast and announcing to the hotel staff and everyone else within earshot that Holmes was indisposed and not to be disturbed, I found him gone. When he did not return that evening, I began to worry that something was a amiss in his plan. This anxiety was so perplexing that I had difficulty in going to sleep. When I succeeded at last, I was awakened by the sound of a woman's voice that I can only describe as otherworldly. Seeming to emanate from behind a tapestry-covered wall, it said, "You must help me, Mr. Holmes. Clear my name!"

Tapping on the wall, I demanded, "Who's in there? Who are you?"

There was no response.

Eager to report this occurrence to Holmes, I expected him

to return in the morning. When he did not, and sent no message, I became increasingly concerned. By late afternoon, my fear for his safety was so acute that I decided to go to the Ministry of Justice and inform Commissioner Krasznadar about all that had transpired. To my astonishment as I entered his office, Holmes was there. Dressed like a peasant, with a pallid face beneath a scruffy beard and holding a gray wig, he exclaimed, "Watson, you arrive at a propitious moment. I was about to tell our friend here what I've learned about the revolutionary plot that's had him so worried that he conceived of a brilliant plan to obtain my assistance without having to do so officially."

"Plan? What plan?"

"Take a seat, Watson. Have you got the little notebook that you always carry at home?"

"I do, but first there is something you should know. Last night in our hotel room I heard a strange voice from inside the wall. There must be a passageway."

"Undoubtedly. The woman's voice was that of the former actress who is now the wife of the commissioner of police. She also wrote the note we found under the door. This was a means of luring me into an investigation. Interrupt me if I am in error on any point, Commissioner."

"You're doing very well so far, Mr. Holmes. Please continue."

"In order to further stimulate my interest in the matter of the revolutionary movement of which Lily Rainer is, indeed, a central figure—"

"Just a moment, Holmes," said I. "You said that Miss Rainer *is*. You mean *was*."

"The lady is alive and well, Watson, and will soon to be under arrest again, along with the mastermind of the plot to overthrow the monarchy."

"Great scot! You've discovered his identity?"

"Brace yourself, my friend. He is none other than the Crown Prince Stefano Wilhelm Yosephus Constantine. That is why he took command of the firing squad. It's the custom in such executions that only one rifle is loaded with a bullet. The others contain blanks. This assures that no member of the squad knows who actually fired the fatal shot. Only the man in charge of the execution knows, because he loads the rifles. He is also the one who administers the coup de grace with a pistol, in this instance, also loaded with blanks. He then sees to disposing of the body. Am I correct, Commissioner?"

"I have long suspected His Highness. What is your direct evidence against him?"

"The leader of the rebels is a man named Josef. One of the Prince's names is a variation, Yosephus. Confident of being above suspicion, he was able to act in complete safety and without question, including making it possible for Lily Rainer to travel in and out of Kazanlak freely. He is also in love with her."

"This is incredible, Holmes. Why should Prince Stefano wish to destroy a throne that he would one day inherit?"

"It's that old bugaboo that has led other men to their downfall. Love, Watson. As the monarch, he could not legally marry the woman he loved. The young man is also infected with the spirit of democracy, picked up when he was a student in America."

"If he didn't wish to be the monarch, he could abdicate."

"In that case," interjected Commissioner Krasznadar, "his brother Rudolfo would be the successor. We would then have a despot. He would certainly provoke a violent revolution."

"This is impossible," I objected. "You can't arrest a prince."

"When Prince Alexei is informed of these facts, I believe that will not be necessary. I am confident that he can be shown the wisdom of breaking with tradition by issuing a decree that he wishes his successor to be the third of his children. The Princess Royal Alexandra is beloved by everyone in Kazanlak. The promise of her succession will take the steam out of revolution."

"I have a question for you, Commissioner," I said. "Did you have three men follow us?"

"They were the prince's men. I know this because I had them followed."

"You did this because you were suspicious of the prince?"

"Yes. But how does one investigate the heir to the throne?"

"You turn to Sherlock Holmes."

Grinning, the commissioner replied, "Exactly!"

"What will you do about the revolutionaries in the meantime?"

"Round them up, of course. As I'm sure Mr. Holmes discovered after he gave my men the slip yesterday, there are not that many. How may the government of Kazanlak reward you for all that you've done for us, Mr. Holmes?"

"For Dr. Watson's sake, you can pledge that Lily Rainer will not again stand before a Ministry of Justice firing squad."

"I can arrange that, sir."

"Because no one was actually harmed by activities of the small number of rebels, I hope that neither will any of them be executed."

"It's not the Balkan way of doing things," said the commissioner with a wry mile, "but you have my word, sir."

"Thank you. I've had my fill of haunting."

· 7 ·

The Adventure of the Stuttering Ghost

*I*n detailed notes that I assembled in order to record the adventures of Sherlock Holmes, initially for my own amusement and eventually for the benefit of posterity, there are no less than fifteen instances in which he had the occasion to employ or comment on the nature of the animal that has rightly been esteemed throughout history as man's best friend. He regarded the dog as so significant in his career that he gave serious thought to writing a small monograph on the subject of uses of canines in the work of the detective.

To Holmes, observation of dogs provided insights into the humans who owned them. As he investigated the astonishing behavior of the famous physiologist Presbury he asserted, "A dog reflects the family life. Whoever saw a frisky dog in a gloomy family, or a sad dog in a happy one? Snarling people have snarling dogs, dangerous people have dangerous ones. Passing moods of dogs often reflect the passing mood of others."

At the head of my list in the category of engaging a dog in a case is a persevering hound named Toby. Without his sensitive nose the affair of the Agra Treasure in my account titled *The Sign of the Four* might not have reached its dramatic conclusion. An ugly, long-haired, lop-eared creature, Toby was a brown and white half spaniel, half lurcher, with a clumsy, waddling gate, owned by a man named Sherman. Taxidermist by trade, he was a colorful keeper of a menagerie that he rented from No. 3 Pinchin Lane.

Second in importance to solving a case was a dog that attracted Holmes's attention because it did not bark in the nighttime. In the investigation of the missing three-quarter, Holmes had the help of a sagacious draghound with the illustrious name Pompey. Devotion of dogs to owners was a vital clue in the adventure of Shoscombe Old Place.

Third on my list of memorable dogs encountered in Holmes's cases was a delightful spaniel belonging to Dr. James Mortimer. I rate it high not because of any importance in the matter of the Hound of the Baskervilles, but because it gave Holmes an opportunity to instruct me yet again on the importance of observation. The country physician had absentmindedly left behind his handsome walking stick in our lodgings in Baker Street after he'd found that Holmes was not in. Examining the cane, Holmes noted among other facts about Mortimer that he owned a small dog. When the doctor returned, he was accompanied by a curly-haired spaniel.

These remembrances of dogs in Holmes's cases are prelude to an adventure involving an especially animated and noisy one. It began with Holmes sorting the morning's delivery of a thick bundle of letters, telegrams, and other messages soliciting his unique services. Most of the missives were discarded because he deemed the matters trivial. Others might be set aside for consideration. A few would be retained if they bore interesting postmarks or a unique cancellation or other characteristic that might contribute to a monograph he intended to write on the distinction of postal markings and varieties of ink.

Looking up from my newspaper, I asked, "Is there anything of interest in the first post?"

"Only one item," he replied. "We are told to expect a visitor this afternoon. The writer states, 'I shall present my problem to you at three o'clock on Wednesday.'"

"That's all there is?"

"It is signed 'Ferdinand.' What does that suggest to you?"

Casting aside my newspaper, I exclaimed excitedly, "Royalty! Reigning monarchs sign papers with just their first names."

"The only King Ferdinand I am aware of died a year ago, and the script is a woman's."

"This Ferdinand, whoever he is, dictated it to a secretary."

"No. The signature is in the same hand."

"A woman named Ferdinand? Extraordinary."

"That is one reason the note was not discarded immediately. The other is this woman's presumption that on such short notice I would adjust my schedule to suit hers."

For several hours, Holmes lost himself in peering through a microscope and studying the postmarks of the letters he'd disdained and I ventured an account of his most recent case. It had taken us to Devonshire and involved the problem of a lifeguard, a calabash pipe, and a dying nursemaid. Our quiet activities ceased precisely at three in the afternoon with the shrill barking of a dog. It grew louder as the person we were anticipating was accompanied up the stairs and into our sitting room by Mrs. Hudson.

Commonplace in appearance, the woman carried a Pekinese dog that not only went on barking, but snapped at me when I attempted to pat its head.

"You must forgive, Ferdinand," said the woman. "He's been nervous since I told him that he would be meeting the famous Sherlock Holmes. You did receive his note?"

"We received *a* note," said I.

"I am Mrs. Jean Frampton, of the Buckinghamshire Framptons. The note wasn't actually written by Ferdinand, of course. He dictated it to me."

"Dictated? Preposterous!"

With a wry smile, Holmes asked, "Why was Ferdinand writing to a detective concerning whatever his problem may be, and not to a veterinarian?"

Ferdinand's response to the query was another outburst of barks.

"I'm afraid he's heard you and was offended Mr. Holmes," said the woman brusquely. "When he is in such an agitated state, the only thing that will calm him is being taken out for a walk. Might I impose on Dr. Watson to do so?"

"Walk your dog, madam?" I said indignantly. "Certainly not!"

"If you wish to consult with me alone, say so, Mrs. Frampton," Holmes interjected, "and Dr. Watson will leave us. As to walking the dog, I believe our conversation will proceed better without the accompaniment of barking."

Feeling foolish, I took the dog from the woman's arms and held its squirming body as she attached a leash to its collar. When I left them alone, my offense at being required to carry out the task of keeping a Pekinese company was assuaged only by my confidence that Holmes would relate to me the substance of the woman's business presently. Meanwhile, I endured not only a tedious stroll up one side of Baker Street and down the opposite, but being accosted by a persistent beggar. Insisting that I buy a box of matches, he dogged me every step of the way until I saw Mrs. Frampton leave 221B Baker Street. At that moment, he ceased hounding me and quickly strode off, while the woman entered a waiting hansom and sped away.

Left with the dog, I leashed it to the hall stand in the foyer of 221B and bounded up the stairs. Furious at the woman for having forgotten the animal, I burst into the sitting room and to my shock discovered Holmes seated at his desk, gagged with a handkerchief and handcuffed to the chair. When I freed him, he calmly inquired, "Did you enjoy your walk, Watson? Tell me about the person who accompanied you."

"He was a particularly noisome beggar selling match boxes, but how did you know I—?"

"We were both taken in by that woman, old man. Your beggar's job was to keep you out of the way while Mrs. Frampton drew a pistol, had me handcuff myself to this chair, gagged me and went through my old case files. Fortunately, she did not think to blindfold me, allowing me to observe that she went through folders under the letters H, R, and S. Do they mean anything to you, Watson?"

"There must be dozens of such folders."

"True, but the combination of H, R, and S suggest that the woman was interested in the case of Randal Rogier. His accomplice was Stuttering Steve Hacker. Eight years ago, they stole the famous—"

"Shroesbury Emeralds!"

"Rogier and Hacker were arrested separately a few days later and both died in Dartmoor Prison. Rogier was stabbed to death by an inmate. Hacker died a few days after suffering a heart attack three weeks ago. Aware that he was dying, he asked to speak with me in the Dartmoor Prison hospital."

"Whatever for?"

"In a last pitiful cock-a-doodle-do, he overcame his pain and managed to stammer that he was taking the secret of the hiding place of the emeralds to the grave, and that unless I was able to communicate with a stuttering ghost, I would die knowing I'd been outsmarted. He also said that he'd outwitted Rogier and the others the day after the robbery by moving the emeralds from Rogier's hiding place to a new one. The jewels were never found. The two other accomplices, a man and woman, got away It's obvious that the person who called herself Mrs. Frampton was one of them and believes that my case files may contain clues concerning the whereabouts of the emeralds. Unfortunately, she took the folders."

"That may be," said I, "but she didn't get away with the notes I made on the case."

"Watson, you are a godsend! I once said that you while are not yourself luminous, you are a conductor of light. Today, you have again shown that I would be lost without my Boswell."

Inspired by Holmes's vast archive of case files, catalogs of seemingly pointless data and an alphabetized conglomeration of information which he lovingly called the "good old index," I had arranged my notes of our shared adventures in similar fashion by the names of the persons involved, dates, locations, and subjects. The material on the theft of the emeralds was arranged accordingly. After gleaning the material under persons' names to no avail, Holmes turned his attention to the locations associated with the Rogier case.

Drawing a card from the file, he exclaimed, "Gaunt's Castle. Do you recall it, Watson?"

"I recall that a man named Gaunt bought a rundown place to create a third-rate imitation of Madame Tussaud's wax works. There was also a hideous simulation of the ruins of the Roman Forum and a series of cellars made to look like the catacombs of Rome where Christians hid out in the time of the Emperor Nero's persecutions."

"You remember it well. Jezra Gaunt was and remains a shadowy figure. I suspected he was associated with the Rogier gang, but was unable to prove it, even after he and Hacker were arrested there. Although I was certain they had hidden the emeralds somewhere in the castle, a search by Inspector Lestrade's men was unavailing. The only item found on Rogier and Hacker was a scrap of paper containing a series of numbers and letters, presumably a code."

"If I jotted them down, they will be in my codes file," I said, "along with the dancing men figures in the Hilton Cubitt tragedy, the Von Bork ciphers, the Red Circle matter, and the Birlstone case."

"In the latter instance, I boasted that I am able to read many ciphers as readily as I plumb the apocrypha of the daily agony columns of newspapers, but the Rogier code stumped me."

Finding the perplexing jumble of letters and numbers in the file, I handed the paper on which I'd jotted them to Holmes. He read aloud, "T2N3O2S5O."

"I thought at the time that the letters and numbers represented the combination of a safe," I said, "or directions, as in the Musgrave Ritual, with the N meaning north and the S south, but the T left me baffled."

Slipping the card into his vest pocket, Holmes asked, "I

know it's getting close to tea time, but can you forgo Mrs. Hudson's scones and clotted cream in the interest of our taking an impromptu tour of Gaunt's Castle?"

"What question! Of course I can."

"Our first stop will be Scotland Yard to inform Lestrade that the Shroesbury Emeralds case has suddenly come alive. There's a dangerous game afoot against a clever opponent, my friend, requiring pistols for both of us and a pocket tape measure."

"It's been eight years. Gaunt may have gone out of business."

"Jezra Gaunt may be gone, but I think it highly unlikely that the British government has allowed a five-hundred-year-old castle to be torn down."

On the way down the stairs, we encountered Mrs. Hudson carrying a tray laden with the accouterments of high tea and observing us with an angry glare.

"I'm sorry, Mrs. Hudson," said I, "but we've no time for refreshments, and would you look after a small dog that you'll find leashed to the stand in the vestibule?"

As Holmes and I passed the animal, it commenced a barking that persisted as we hailed a passing hansom and Holmes asked the driver, "Do you know if Gaunt's Castle is still open for business, cabby?"

"It was as of last week, but I can't say how much longer it will be. It's so out of the way that hardly anybody goes there these days. Rather than take the time getting there and back, the people on holiday prefer Madame Tussaud's."

"There's a stop I must make on the way. Scotland Yard, please."

Upon our arrival, Holmes said, "I'll be but a moment, Watson, Stay here and keep an eye out for anyone who might be following us."

When we reached Gaunt's Castle as a yellowish dusk was fading, only one light burned on the ground floor of the dreary ancient structure. After several loud raps on the door, it opened slowly and we were greeted by old Jezra Gaunt himself. "I'm sorry, gentlemen," he declared, "but we're closed for the day."

Placing a hand on the door, I said insistently, "This gentleman is Sherlock Holmes."

The name evoked a gasp from Gaunt.

"We are not here to engage in sightseeing," I continued forcefully. "It's a matter of the utmost importance that we see the catacombs and we demand admittance."

"Well, if it's that important, by all means come in."

Entering a dim foyer, Holmes asked, "Has anyone been here recently who also expressed an interest in only seeing the catacombs?"

"Now that you mention it, a woman and a man came a few days ago. Very pushy they was. They were down in the cellars the longest time. She told me she was interested in buying the property. Even though I informed her it wasn't for sale, she went about measuring."

For the first hour in the glow of flickering gas lamps, Holmes explored a series of cavelike spaces to no avail. When we came to the deepest of them, I noticed in the beam above the entrance a faded painting of a knight in full Crusader array. "If my memory serves," I said as we went into the small chamber, "this castle was once the headquarters of a group of Templars after they were driven out of France when the king got tired of being in debt to them. They claimed to have started Freemasonry in Britain, an assertion that is much in dispute."

"Your knowledge of the trivia of the history of England

never ceases to amaze me. You should consider abandoning your obsession with romanticizing my cases for the readers of *The Strand* magazine and write book on the subject."

"I mention the Templars who used this castle only because I saw a picture of one at the entrance this room. They were consecrated to St. Antony, but their choice of their symbol was unique, in that the red cross on their white robes had the beam at the top of the shaft, rather like a capital T, whereas the common depiction of a crucifix has the cross beam lower on the shaft and in the shape of the lower-case letter t."

"Watson, if I ever again question the time you spend in Masonic Lodge meetings," said Holmes, "feel free to shut me up by uttering the name St. Antony! You've solved the code! The key is the first letter. The cross in the carving over the door to this room in the shape of a T is the spot from which we must begin measuring "

"The first number after the T," I said excitedly as I looked at the code, "is two, followed by the letter N. It's either two paces or two feet, perhaps two yards, to the north. Then thirty paces to the——. Wait. This makes no sense. The thirty is followed by the number two and the letter S. The code doesn't say in what direction to measure off the thirty. There should be a letter E for east or a W for west."

Plucking the code from my hand, Holmes studied it in the torch light, then exclaimed, "I have it! These directions are written in Randal Rogier's first language. French. The O in the code stands for 'ouest.' We go three west! And not three paces, three feet or three yards, Watson. We must also measure in the French way. By *meters.*"

"Unfortunately, the pocket tape measure we brought is marked in feet."

"Have you forgotten your schoolboy mathematics? One meter equals 3.28 feet. It's a simple calculation. What we'll need that we didn't bring is a spade. Ask Gaunt to lend us his."

As I turned to leave the cavernlike room to fetch him, a woman's voice from out of the darkness beyond the entrance said, "Thank you for your efforts, Mr. Holmes, but my friends and I will take over the search for the emeralds from here."

"Good evening, Mrs. Frampton. I was wondering when you would show yourself. May I offer my compliments on the execution of your plan? When you failed in your exploration a few days ago, you decided to employ me to find them for you. Very clever of you."

"It's high praise, indeed, coming from you."

"Yes, but now I must disappoint you. It's true that I've led you to place where Rogier hid the emeralds, but Watson and I did not come here alone. I saw immediately that the purpose of your visit to Baker Street was to rekindle my interest in the case of the Shroesbury Emeralds in the hope that I would lead you to them. You didn't blindfold me so that I'd see which of the files you were taking. Anticipating our meeting, I made a stop en route, as Dr. Watson can attest."

"At Scotland Yard!"

"Amazingly," Holmes continued, "Inspector Lestrade grasped the situation. The police by now have this castle surrounded. There's one other thing you should know, madam. I paid a visit to Harker at Dartmoor Prison three weeks ago. At that time I asked the warden if anyone had visited him recently. He reported that a woman had done so the previous week. For that reason, your call at Baker Street was not unexpected. By the way, the jewels are not here in this room and haven't been since the day after the robbery. Hacker moved them to another spot, the location of which he took to the grave with him."

"The dirty stammering rat!"

"Listen! Do you hear that?"

"I don't hear nothing except you prattling on."

"That's odd. I was certain I heard the laughter of a stuttering ghost."

With the owner of the Pekinese and her cohort in crime, a scoundrel named Alfie Smith, sentenced to prison for the robbery of the emeralds, the remaining problem in the case was what to do with the woman's dog. To my surprise and consternation, this dilemma was resolved, and the peace and tranquility of 221B Baker Street shattered, by Mrs. Hudson's announcement that she found it enchanting and had decided to adopt the most ill-tempered and noisiest canine I had ever encountered.

· 8 ·

The Clue of the Hungry Cat

On a dismally gray, cold, and damp Wednesday afternoon in late December of 1895, I paused in my writing for want of the right adjective, to gaze absently through the window and found that a dense fog had enveloped Baker Street. Except for a faint yellow light in an upper window of the house opposite 221B, from which Colonel Sebastian Moran had attempted to assassinate Sherlock Holmes with an ingenious air rifle, all the familiar buildings seemed to have vanished. On just such a day a few weeks earlier Holmes had been engaged by his brother Mycroft in the matter of the murder of Arthur Cadogan West. The Woolrich Arsenal clerk's body had been found miles away on the Underground railway with some top secret drawings for the Bruce-Partington submarine in his pockets.

Like that day while we awaited the arrival of his mysterious brother, Holmes was in a restive mood. The floor around his chair was strewn with the morning newspapers, thrown down impatiently with the protest, "Dull, dull, dull! Even the agony columns are boring. The only item of interest is the trial of Robert Saunders for the murder of the wife of his former employer in the course of a robbery. Eight pounds were taken from a cash box that contained sixty-five. I ask you, how many thieves do you know who would take eight pounds and leave the rest?"

"If the man is charged," said I, "the Crown must have convincing evidence against him."

"The only person to appear in court for the defense was the girl Saunders is engaged to marry, Helen Caldwell. Hardly an unbiased witness. Despite her poignant pleas on Saunders' behalf, I have no doubt he will be found guilty. Inspector Davis was a powerful witness. But the crime itself makes no sense. To murder a woman for eight pounds, then set the house on fire in an attempt to obscure what happened? Ludicrous! The entire trial has been a travesty of hearsay and circumstantial evidence."

"If you feel so strongly, why haven't you done anything about it?"

"The murder occurred in Sudbury while I was occupied with a host of other matters, including the case of the submarine plans," he answered as he came to the window next to my desk. "The painful truth, old friend, is that there are so many crimes in this city that Scotland Yard has a hard time keeping up with them. It's only in the difficult ones that they turn to me, and then with reluctance."

Parting the curtain, Holmes gazed pensively down at the street. He had done so on the day Mycroft had sent a telegram stating that he would come round to seek Holmes's assistance in the Cadogan West affair. On that foggy morning, he had stated wistfully, "See how the figures loom up, are dimly seen, and then blend once more into the cloud-bank. The thief or murderer could roam London on such a day as the tiger does the jungle, unseen until he pounces, and then evident only to his victim."

Having learned that when he was in such a ruminative mood that silence on my part was a prudent policy, I returned my attention to writing, and he went back to his chair.

"The first I heard of the Saunders case," he said after a few minutes, "was when the trial began on Monday at the Old Bailey before Justice Hardwick."

An austere and grimly visaged judge, he was known to barristers around the courthouse as Hanging Harry, which boded ill for the hapless Mr. Saunders.

The day passed with no abeyance in the inclement weather or the restless, gray mood that gripped Holmes when he was idle. When Mrs. Hudson served a hearty dinner of one of his favorite meals, shepherd's pie, for which he usually lauded what he called her fine Scottish cooking, he barely touched it. On such a dreary evening, I expected him to serenade me with two or three of his melancholy violin compositions, but his Stradivarius remained in its open case in a corner. Slouched in a chair, he smoked three pipes without uttering a word, then bolted to his feet and declared, "This man Saunders had the benefit of good education and shows every sign of exceptional intelligence, yet he stupidly and brutally killed Mrs. Post to conceal a minor theft of money that he claims he was owed by his former employer, a contention that was confirmed from the witness box by Mr. Post. A local public house keeper cited an argument between them about the money in front of a dozen witnesses."

"Mrs. Post might have heard Saunders and confronted him. Realizing she could identify him, he panicked."

"Nay. She could not have heard any intruder According to the newspaper accounts, the woman was stone deaf from birth."

"Really? I seem to have missed that fact."

"The press has its uses, Watson. While today's journalists magnify the sensational, they are commendably diligent in presenting unvarnished data. Three of the popular sheets provided detailed biographies of the central personalities in the Saunders case. He is a hardworking man with no criminal record. He and Miss Caldwell became engaged five months ago. Mrs. Amanda Post was rather well off financially through an inheritance from her father, the founder of the textile firm now run by Mr. Post. By all accounts, he is an Australian by birth and appears to have been in business in the city of Adelaide."

Feeling at liberty to engage Holmes on the matter, I ventured, "As to the money left behind by Saunders, it might have been in large notes that could have been traced by the police."

"Were I Saunders, I would surely realize after the public argument that taking only the eight pounds and leaving the rest would be as conclusive as fingerprints. If all the money were missing, I could make a plausible argument that the theft could have been committed by anyone. I would have taken all the notes and burned the traceable ones."

"Most criminals are not as logical as you, Holmes. If they were, Scotland Yard would not enjoy its vaunted reputation."

"I grant you that our friends in the Criminal Division of the Metropolitan Police tend to be a sorry lot, but I do not count Inspector Davis among them. I attribute his actions in this matter to the common failing of policemen. They jump to a conclusion and stick to it regardless of the obvious flaws in the theory. And the consequences. One of the most egregious examples was the arrest of Horner for the theft of the Blue Carbuncle, when closer examination of the circumstances would have indicated the possibility that Horner had been set up."

"This Saunders affair has really nettled you."

"What nettles me is indifference to logic!"

"The case goes to the jury tomorrow morning. Whatever you might do for Saunders will be too late. And you could be wrong."

"Whether I'm wrong or right is not the issue. Uncertainty is what keeps me awake. I need data, Watson. In that cause, I propose an early breakfast and a trip to Sudbury."

Accordingly, we left behind the fog of London on the first train and arrived in welcome sunlight. Gazing at the burned ruin of the Post residence, I said, "The murder occurred weeks ago, Holmes. I fail to see what you hope to find in this awful wreckage."

"I'm interested in the neighbors, Watson. Nothing can be as enlightening for a detective as the person who lives next door or across the street at the scene of the crime. In this instance, I think we should start with the woman who's watching us from her parlor window."

The name on the letter box was Mrs. Doris Roberts. As Holmes was about to knock, the door opened narrowly. "If you gentlemen are from the newspapers," said a woman's voice, "I'm tired of being bothered. If you're salesmen, I'm not interested."

"We are neither, madam. I am Sherlock Holmes."

The door swung wide open to reveal a matronly woman with silver-gray hair and wearing a gray apron over a flowery dress.

"Oh my," she said excitedly, "This is a genuine honor. Do I take it correctly that this gentleman is Dr. Watson?"

"You do, madam," said I.

"If you don't mind my saying so, you're a very good writer. I do enjoy reading a good mystery story, which is how I know about both of you. Have you come about the tragedy in the house opposite?"

"We have, Mrs. Roberts," Holmes replied "May we come in?"

"Certainly. Pardon the look of the place. This is my cleaning up day, you see. I was doing the parlor when I chanced to see you looking at the burned-out house. Make yourselves at home and ask me whatever questions come to mind."

"The first," said Holmes as we settled into the small but cheery parlor, "is why you were not called upon to testify at Robert Saunders' trial?"

"The inspector who investigated told me that my going to court would not be required because the police had all the evidence against that fellow Saunders they needed. In the light of what he said, I'm surprised that you are here, Mr. Holmes."

"I have not come on behalf of the police. Please tell us about the night of the murder."

"Please understand that I am not a busybody. I tend my own business, but what with that poor blind woman being home alone when her husband was away on business, I kept an eye on the house for who was coming and going and that sort of thing, especially any salesmen who might try to take advantage of her."

"That was very kind of you, Mrs. Roberts," I replied. "You are a good neighbor."

"Quite, " said Holmes. "What did you observe on the day in question?"

"That morning, Mr. Post was going away on business, as

usual. Amanda had told me he was going to Brighton and would be gone a few days. I saw him standing at the front door and waving good-bye to her a little before seven in the morning."

"Did you see her wave back to him?"

"Well not exactly. But I noticed the curtain in the parlor window moving. The next thing to attract my attention happened around eight o'clock that evening. I heard a scratching on the kitchen door, and when I opened it, there was Mrs. Post's cat, Minnie, mewing and mewing like she was hungry, which struck me as odd because Amanda Post was particular about feeding Minnie at six o'clock. Anyway, I put down a saucer of milk on the stoop and went to bed. A few hours later, me and Eddie, my husband, were awakened by the sounds of the fire brigade."

"At what time?"

"Just after midnight. Naturally, I was worried about Amanda. I told the fire brigade's captain that she was deaf, but the fire was raging so bad that no one could go inside. Her body wasn't found until morning, and you could have knocked me over with a feather when Chief Constable Harris told me that she was dead. She'd been strangled in her bed!"

"Thank you, Mrs. Roberts," said Holmes abruptly. "You've been very helpful."

Upon leaving the house, I said to Holmes, "I don't see anything helpful in what she had to tell us."

"The hungry cat, Watson. Very illuminating!"

"What do you propose to do now, speak with the local chief constable?"

"That would be a waste of time. I prefer a chat with the captain of the fire brigade."

While Holmes's relationship with Scotland Yard and various provincial police officials was often strained, leaving him with a jaundiced view of them and their work, he held the men who battled fires with intense respect. "Firemen are the bravest people on earth," he remarked upon reading of a daring rescue by a pair of fire fighters of three members of a family trapped by flames in an upper floor of a house. "When everyone else is running from an inferno, they run toward it." In two of his most notable cases, *The King of Bohemia Affair* and *The Adventure of the Norwood Builder,* he had used a faked alarm of fire to achieve the goals of locating a letter and unmasking a murderer and clearing the name of a young lawyer whom Inspector Lestrade had arrested for the crime of murdering the very person Holmes forced out of hiding.

A sturdy, homespun embodiment of the character of men of the fire brigades, Captain Jonathan Wiley was as surprised to find himself in the presence of Sherlock Holmes as Mrs. Roberts. On the question of the cause of the fire that destroyed the Post house, he was adamant that it had not been accidental. "It was set all, right," he said. "When we arrived, it was blazing like a bonfire on Guy Fawkes Day. I knew it was deliberate by the smell of kerosene."

"Yet you found the cash box intact."

"Fires do strange things. Another object that survived was an alarm clock on a bureau next to that poor woman's bed. The bureau was nearly burned to a crisp, and there was nothing left of the lady's corset that was on it. All I found of it was a few wires. But the clock was intact and still ticking. The alarm had been set for half past eleven and gone off. Unfortunately, by that time the woman must have been already dead. I assumed that she had suffocated, until I was told she had been strangled. That's why I kept the things that we found which were intact, in case of their being needed as evidence. All they wanted was the cash box. I must say that I was surprised that they charged Bob Saunders. He was a very nice chap who was always good for standing a friend to a pint at the pub."

"May I see the items from the bedroom, sir?"

"Since the case is done, except for the verdict, I don't see why not."

After poking around in a jumble of charred and sooty articles stored in a small box in the fire brigade office, Holmes asked, "Would it be any trouble to you, Captain Wiley, to hold onto this material until you hear from me, perhaps in a day or two?"

"No trouble at all, Mr. Holmes."

Examinations by Holmes of commonplace items associated with a crime scene always fascinated and mystified observers and frequently left me wondering what he was looking for. In almost every instance, I was content to wait for an explanation, but as we left the fire brigade for the train station, I felt impelled to ask, "What did you expect to learn from that box of rubble?"

"I needed to confirm an extraordinarily interesting observation by Captain Wiley about the clock he found in the bedroom."

"What observation?"

"That it was an alarm clock."

"What is so extraordinary about an alarm clock in a bedroom?"

"Amanda Post was deaf."

"The alarm clock was obviously her husband's."

"You find nothing curious about that, Watson?"

"Not a thing."

"The alarm was set for half past eleven and had gone off. We know from Mrs. Roberts that Post left the house at seven. Why, then, did he set the alarm for eleven-thirty?"

"I fail to see what the clock has to do with this murder."

"Have you given no thought to the wires which Wiley also found?"

"They were the remnants of a burned-up corset."

"According to Captain Wiley, based on a perfectly reasonable expectation on the part of a man who had no idea that a murder had been committed. Thanks to his decision to retain the evidence in this case, I am more confident that ever that Robert Saunders is innocent. But I can do nothing about it until we return to London."

Whatever he had in mind remained there during the train ride and throughout the rest of the day. Holmes's silence was broken late in the afternoon by two incidents. The first, a letter from the earl of Brookfield. Requesting Holmes's assistance. it contained a bank draft for 500 pounds in the form of a retainer.

"You may reply to Lord Brookfield," said Holmes impatiently, "that the paintings he's worried about were sold by his son to buy jewels for the dancer with whom the young man is enamored. and that his bank draft is enclosed."

The second intrusion was a visit by Daniel Post. Not since the arrival in Baker Street of the insufferable Grimesby Roylott in the case of the Speckled Band had anyone stormed into our sitting room in such a furious state. "Upon returning to Sudbury following the conviction of Robert Saunders for the murder of my wife," he seethed as he began pacing the room, "I was informed by Mrs. Roberts that you were asking her questions. I find this outrageous."

"Please sit down, sir," Holmes replied, "and I'll explain."

Continuing to stride back and forth, Post retorted. "I am not interested in explanations. I demand that you cease your inquiries. If you do not, you will hear from my solicitor. Good day to you, sir, and to your equally obnoxious associate. I am not a man to trifle with, gentlemen."

When he was gone, slamming the door on the way out, Holmes turned toward me with a smile and asked, "What did you observe about our visitor's demeanor, Watson?"

"I saw unconscionable rudeness."

"I refer to his constant pacing."

"The man was agitated."

"Did you know that our sitting room is twenty-three feet in length with no obstructions in the area he walked? His strides covered eight feet forward and eight feet back. That distance is the same as the length of a prison cell. I believe we may safely deduce that at some period in Post's life prior to coming to England, he had the occasion to become familiar with at least one prison in Australia. Will you pardon me, Watson, while I compose a cablegram to the prison authorities in Adelaide?"

When a reply was received two days later, Holmes said, "All that remains now is to get Post to offer a confession."

"How do you expect to achieve that?"

"By inviting Mr. Post to call on me so that I may apologize for my behavior the other day, of course. When he comes, as I'm certain he will, have your revolver in your pocket."

Although I doubted that Post would rise to the bait, Holmes again proved to be a better judge of human nature than I. The following day, after a serving of Mrs. Hudson's incomparable high tea, Holmes declared, "I feel I owe you an explanation of my recent actions, Mr. Post, in the form of how I viewed this extraordinary affair."

"I do feel such thing is called for, sir."

"A certain man who for the moment shall remain nameless, meets and courts a wealthy woman, who despite the handicap of being deaf is charming and attractive. They marry, and in desire to inherit her fortune and a lucrative textile firm, he strangles the poor incredulous woman and contrives to point the police toward another man."

"A fanciful story, Mr. Holmes, but that is all it is."

"I am not finished, Mr. Post. I haven't told you how the murder was committed."

"Pure conjecture on your part," said Post, rising from his chair. "I bid you both good day"

"Sit down, sir, and listen, or Dr. Watson may find it necessary to persuade you to do so with his revolver."

"I shall certainly report this outrage to the police."

"I'm sure they will be interested in the plan you devised to kill your wife. It was quite ingenious and carried out almost flawlessly. Knowing that Mrs. Roberts would be watching, you staged a farewell to your wife, who was already dead. You used a length of string attached to a curtain to make it move, giving the appearance that your wife was at the parlor window. You had set the alarm clock for half past eleven in the evening. It was attached to wires, which created a spark that ignited kerosene you had spread throughout the bedroom. The only element you failed to consider was your wife's cat."

"It's you word against mine, Mr. Holmes."

"No, sir, it is the word of Sherlock Holmes against a man who served fifteen years in an Australian prison for business fraud and was suspected of the murder of his wealthy wife. Now, if you wish, you may go to the police and lodge a complaint against me and Watson for illegal imprisonment."

"You surprise me, Mr., Holmes. Did you think I would come here unprepared?"

With that, Post drew a pistol from a coat pocket. Fortunately, he was not as quick on the trigger as I. My bullet struck him in the shoulder before he could fire.

"Well done, Watson," Holmes exclaimed as he rushed to the wounded man and kicked away his pistol. "We now have a reason to summon the police and lodge a charge against you of attempted murder, Mr. Post, that will hold you long enough for me to prove a case of murder and arson. My advice is that you spare everyone the trouble of a trial by confessing. If not, I shall see to it that you stand in the dock in the court of Justice Hardwick, known as Hanging Harry. In the meantime, you will be in the custody of several individuals at Scotland Yard who have a way of dealing with men who take advantage of women with physical handicaps."

"All right, all right," said Post with a groan. "I see that the game is up."

Upon Post's confession that the crimes were committed in the manner Holmes deduced, Robert Saunders was released with an apology on behalf of the Crown. A few days later came a package with a note from Mrs. Roberts informing Holmes that she had adopted Minnie the cat and that the enclosed saucer was the one she had set out with milk.

"I know from reading Dr. Watson's stories that you keep mementos of your cases," she explained, "and I thought you'd care to add to your museum the clue that solved this one."

· 9 ·

The Singular Affair of the Dying Schoolboys

On one occasion as I sat taking notes while a potential client told Sherlock Holmes what had motivated the visit to our consulting room, I found myself wondering what the late Dorsetshire businessman and real estate speculator Edward Berkeley Portman might say if he suddenly materialized and learned that the parcel of land numbered 221 in the plan he had laid out for a street in the West End of London and named for his friend Sir Edward Baker had become ranked among the city's most famous addresses. So widely renowned was Holmes that his place of abode had become an attraction to sightseers along with Buckingham Place, No. 10 Downing Street, Covent Garden, the Royal Albert Hall, the British Museum, Trafalgar Square, and Piccadilly Circus, as well as Scotland Yard overlooking the Thames Embankment.

I also pondered from time to time what Mr. Portman and the namesake baronet would think of the nature of the myriad men and women who came seeking Holmes's assistance or his advice. They ranged from an indiscreet monarch dreading a scandal in Bohemia and men who represented the British Crown to a Baker Street commissionaire who found a forsaken Christmas goose with a priceless gem in its crop, a terrified woman cyclist, the arch criminal Moriarty, a young lawyer expecting to be charged with murder, scores of ordinary people in trouble, and a group of boisterous urchins known as the Baker Street Irregulars, led by a scruffy ragamuffin named Wiggins. All climbed the seventeen steps to the first floor suite (for which Mrs. Hudson charged Holmes and myself a princely rent) with confidence that when they left, they had placed their problems in the hands of the world's first and foremost private consulting detective.

On an especially stormy September evening in 1888 during the murderous rampage of Jack the Ripper, the troubled individual who came to present his problem to Holmes was a good-looking, middle-aged example of gentlemanly English society, a man who would have been welcome in the company of Mr. Portman, Lord Baker, and every notable estate owner in England, not only by reason of his reputation, but because Randolph Landers' family name appeared in Burke's Peerage. The second son of the late Lord Louis Landers, he was the nephew of the former, but ailing, distinguished member of Parliament Stanley Landers. The scion of one of the wealthiest lineages in the realm, Randolph Landers, had been in the newspapers recently in connection with his miraculous survival of the ill-fated merchant vessel *Sophie Anderson*. She had been lost at sea in a gale during a voyage from India. Clinging to a spar of the sunken ship, Lord Landers was adrift for days. Washed ashore on a remote island, he was marooned for more than two years.

"The result of my being presumed dead in that calamity," Landers explained as prelude to elucidating the reason for calling upon Holmes, "was that my young brother Eric inherited the estate and the guardianship of our uncle. Upon my arrival, I learned that Eric had died one year earlier at his school in Wales on the moors near Cardiff."

Stirring in his chair, Holmes asked, "The name of the school?"

"Ponsonby Hall. It was established a few years ago by Dr. Morgan Ponsonby for the purpose of taking in problem boys of well-to-do families."

"What sort of problem boys?"

"Some had physical disabilities. Most were behavioral challenges."

"Your brother's problem?"

"Eric was sent there by my uncle for the latter reason."

"The cause of your brother's demise?"

"Dr. Ponsonby's death certificate stated that he died of pneumonia."

"Why do you doubt it?"

"My brother was a healthy lad who had never been ill in his life."

"Your brother's age?"

"He was thirteen."

"What were the behavioral problems that persuaded your uncle to send him there?"

"As far as I can tell, Eric was a typical thirteen-year-old."

"What did you find when you investigated the circumstances of Eric's death during your visit to Ponsonby Hall?"

"I don't recall saying that I went to the school."

All but leaping to his feet, Holmes exclaimed, "My dear man, you came to consult with me. Therefore, you must have learned something to raise your suspicions, and where could that have happened except at Ponsonby Hall? How long were you in Wales?"

"Two days."

"What is it that you gleaned from your questioning of Dr. Ponsonby that impelled you to see me on this matter?"

"I never did talk to Dr. Ponsonby. I was told that the man was too ill to receive callers."

"Told by whom?"

"I spoke to a frightfully intimidating matron named Mrs. Arkwright."

"Then what did you do?"

"I decided to bring the facts to you."

"Obviously! I refer to the time you spent in Wales after your visit to Ponsonby Hall. I do not believe you simply took in the local historical landmarks,"

"I made inquiries in the nearby village."

"What did you learn during your inquiries that persuaded you to call upon me?"

"The school has a black name among the villagers. Five boys have died there in the last two years under circumstances similar to my brother's."

"Have you discussed this with your uncle?"

"He died of a heart attack in February."

"Please accept Dr. Watson's and my condolences."

"Thank you, but I've spent no time mourning his death. I hold him responsible for what happened to Eric. As surely as I'm sitting here, Mr. Holmes, my brother was murdered so that Uncle Stanley would inherit the estate. That plan went awry, of course, when he discovered that I survived the sinking of the *Sophie Anderson*."

Looking up from my notebook, I interjected, "With respect, sir, this is England. Boys are not routinely murdered at school, inheritances notwithstanding."

"Patriotic feelings aside, Watson," Holmes retorted, "the location of a private school in a desolate spot could provide excellent, profitable opportunities for removing unwanted relatives. If these shocking occurrences have been taking place at Ponsonby Hall, we may be able to keep them from being repeated. Lord Landers, can you meet Watson and me at Paddington Station at the West of England train platform tomorrow morning?"

"Nothing is more important to me, sir, than getting to the bottom of this."

Taking down Bradshaw's compendium of railway schedules from a shelf of reference books, Holmes handed me the thick, dog-eared volume and said, "Look up the departure times, please, Watson."

With an agreement to meet at half past seven and Lord Landers barely down the stairs, Holmes had his index of medical practitioners open. "Ponsonby," he declared. "Born in Cardiff in 1848. Graduated from the Arizona Territory Medical College in 1869 and served in the army hospital in Calcutta, India. Listen to this, Watson! 'He was later associated in private practice in that city for two years with Dr. Grimesby Roylott.' "

"Great heavens. There's a macabre coincidence!"

"As I said at the time of the Stoke Moran business, when a doctor goes wrong he is the first among criminals," said Holmes said as he slammed closed the directory. "When you pack your bag, include your trusty revolver."

When we stepped from the West England Express at Cardiff exactly on schedule, Lord Landers advised, "The school is about six miles east of here."

"Before going there," Holmes said, "I have a few questions for the village undertaker."

Upon locating the mortuary in the hamlet, I thought for a moment that we had somehow found ourselves projected into a story by Charles Dickens, an author known for assigning his characters odd or whimsical names. Scarcely believing my eyes as I gazed at the name on the sign in the window of the undertaking establishment, I could not help chuckling when I read, "Llewellyn Coffin."

My amusement continued, though to myself, when I laid eyes on the tall, slender, and gaunt proprietor. Dressed in a long black morning coat with gray striped trousers and spats, he was like a caricature of a mortician one would expect to find in *Punch* or some other humor magazine.

"Good afternoon, gentlemen," he said solemnly. "I am Llewellyn Coffin. How may I be of service in your hour of bereavement?"

"That is not our purpose, sir," said Holmes. "We are interested in obtaining information on the deaths in the past two years at Ponsonby Hall. Were you engaged by Dr. Ponsonby in making the final arrangements?"

"I was, and I assure you that everything was conducted properly."

"Did you perform the autopsies on the boys?"

"Who are you, sir," said Mr. Coffin indignantly, "and why is this any of your business? Are you from the police?"

"I am Sherlock Holmes. I act independently of the police. These men are Dr. John H. Watson and Lord Landers. His brother died at the Ponsonby Hall last December."

"Oh yes. My condolences, Your Lordship. The cause was pneumonia, as I recall."

"How can you be sure," asked Lord Landers, "if there was no autopsy?"

"I had a death certificate signed by Dr. Ponsonby. I was in no position to question it. I handle all the funerals for the school, you see."

"In preparing the bodies for interment," Holmes asked, did you note anything peculiar?"

"Excuse me, Mr. Holmes, but I'm not sure I should be discussing this with you."

"It's I or answer to the police. Your reply suggests that you did find something unusual."

"It was the look on those boys' faces. They were as if in their last moments of life they'd had their wits frightened out of them. And there were strange marks on their legs and arms, as though they had been bitten by a very small dog."

Remembering that the instrument of death in the Dr. Roylott affair at Stoke Moran had been a Swamp Adder, I asked, "Might they have been snake bites?"

"They were similar, but there were too many. That's why I thought they were made by a small dog, or perhaps a large cat."

Turning toward the door, Holmes said, "Thank you, Mr. Coffin. Good day to you."

"I trust you won't tell Dr. Ponsonby about this conversation."

"You have my word on that, sir. However, you may find yourself with less business from him in the future."

As Holmes lit a pipe on the sidewalk, I asked, "Where to now? Ponsonby Hall?"

"If Lord Landers will take us to the inn where he stayed, I intend to compose and send a telegram to Jonas Appleton of the British Museum. As to Ponsonby Hall, I'm dispatching you in the guise of a wealthy Scotsman. You will inquire about enrolling a troublesome young cousin. I leave it to you to insinuate in your meeting with the headmaster that you would not be distressed if the lad were to suddenly fall ill and die."

"Why me? You're the one who was an actor in your youth and are a master of disguise."

"It's perfect casting. Lord Landers, do I in any way resemble a rich man from Scotland?"

"Not in the least, Mr. Holmes."

"Then the matter is settled. While you carry out your masquerade and I wait for a reply to my telegram. I shall follow another line of investigation. Who shall you be, Watson?"

"As it happens, I was in medical school in Edinburgh with an Aberdeen laddie named Angus McLaughlin. Unfortunately for him and fortunately for the people of Scotland, he proved unsuitable for the study of medicine. He became a lawyer. I'll use his name and background."

A gray stone structure rising with grim solidity atop a craggy hill in the desolate and gloomy expanse of the moor, Ponsonby Hall presented all the hideous aspects of Dartmoor Prison. This foreboding atmosphere was so evocative of doom that I doubted Mr. Dickens's pen could describe it sufficiently. My sense of despair was deepened by the scowling countenance of the imposing woman who opened the door.

"Who are you," she demanded, "and what is it you want?"

Having become quite convincing in mimicking the Scottish accent while in medical school, I replied, "My name is Angus McLaughlin. I've come down from Scotland to inquire about enrolling my young cousin. I wish to speak with Dr. Ponsonby."

Looking me up and down suspiciously, the woman whom I assumed to be the matron Mrs. Arkwright declared "Enrollment in Ponsonby Hall is quite expensive. It's five thousand pounds per year, plus food and accommodations."

"Madam, I am not concerned about the cost. My cousin Edward has become so trying of late that I'd pay double that amount to be rid of him permanently."

"Wait in the library, sir. Dr. Ponsonby is engaged at the moment with an ill student."

Following her to a large room as cheerless as the Hall, I said, "Nothing serious I hope."

"I'm afraid Carruthers Minor has contracted pneumonia."

"Shouldn't he be taken to hospital?"

"We have a completely equipped infirmary occupying the entire the first floor, and Dr. Ponsonby is an experienced physician."

As I waited in the dim, chilly library and recalled my happy boyhood days at school, I noted that, unlike my own educational institution, Ponsonby Hall was curiously quiet. In the fifteen minutes I sat in a singularly uncomfortable chair, I heard no footsteps nor young voices, with the exception of a muffled crying of a boy that seemed to come from the floor above. Being both a doctor and a literary man, I left my chair to investigate the volumes on the shelves that appeared to have been bought *en masse* from a secondhand book store. Astonishingly, there was a shocking absence of medical tomes. As I wondered if this would be of significance to Holmes, I was interrupted by the entrance Dr. Ponsonby. Expecting to see the embodiment of the sinister exploiter of boys named Fagin in Mr. Dickens' *Oliver Twist*, I found him to be a come-to-life Mr. Macawber straight out of the pages of *David Copperfield*.

"So sorry to have kept you waiting, Mr. McLaughlin," said

he as he crossed the room to a cabinet that he unlocked to reveal well-stocked shelves of wines and stronger distilled spirits. "I hope you are not an abstainer, sir, and will allow me to pour you a glass of sherry."

"There are few abstainers in Scotland, Dr. Ponsonby."

Handing me a brimming glass, he said, 'You have a sense of humor, sir."

"I do indeed, but my cousin has put it to a severe test. I find myself not only regretting that I took him in as guardian after his parents died, but wishing he had perished with them."

"How old is your cousin?"

"Thirteen, going on forty," I replied after a sip of the fine sherry, "and likely to wind up in prison despite his large inheritance. That is, if someone doesn't murder the little devil."

Smiling slyly, Ponsonby replied, "Accidents do happen. And fatal illnesses. We have a lad who at present has a severe case pneumonia. Like you, his parents probably would not be grieved if he shouldn't survive. Mrs. Arkwright has informed me you feel that way about your cousin. She said you even joked that you would pay ten thousand pounds to be rid of him."

"A small price, sir, considering that upon his death, I become the sole beneficiary of a formidable estate."

With a sudden burst of laughter, Ponsonby exclaimed, "My compliments, sir, but not for this story you've been relating so convincingly. I laud your acting ability."

"I beg your pardon?"

"Your fame has preceded you even into Wales, Dr. Watson. Your picture along with that of Sherlock Holmes appeared in a recent Cardiff newspaper article on the subject of Holmes's triumph in the matter of the theft of jewels belonging to the

Prince of Wales. I have no idea why you have come here, sir, but this farce is at an end. Now get out!"

Dejected and feeling humiliated, I reported my failure to Holmes and Lord Landers at the village inn half an hour later.

"Don't blame yourself, old friend," said Holmes. "The fact that Dr. Ponsonby rose to the bait of Angus McLaughlin's willingness to pay ten thousand pounds if his cousin were to die at Ponsonby Hall validates Lord Landers's suspicion that the man and his female accomplice are murderers. All that remains is to confirm their method. They reported that Lord Landers's brother died of pneumonia, but it's the presence of marks on their victims' legs and arms that interests me. They suggest the injection of a type of poison that produces respiratory failure, which in the case of an autopsy could be attributed to pneumonia."

"Good heavens, Holmes. The matron informed me I had to wait to see Ponsonby because he was treating a boy named Carruthers Minor for pneumonia in the first-floor infirmary."

"No doubt he was attending to the boy in a special room at the end of a corridor at the rear of the infirmary that is always kept locked. Only Ponsonby and Arkwright have a key to it."

With a gasp of amazement, Lord Landers asked, "How could you know that, Mr. Holmes? Are you also a clairvoyant?"

"This afternoon as Watson was in the library with Ponsonby I was engaged in pretending to be an itinerant horse groom seeking employment at the school."

Holmes had employed just such a disguise and later masqueraded as a Nonconformist clergyman to force Irene Adler to reveal the hiding place of letters that if made public would have been an embarrassment to the king of Bohemia. On other occasions I had seen Holmes become a common loafer, a denizen of an opium den, an asthmatic master mariner, an old sporting man, and an Irish-American spy.

"I had a delightful conversation with the all-round handyman at Ponsonby Hall by the name of Ned Baxter," Holmes continued. "His wife Emma is the cook and house-keeper. When I stated that I'd heard that the villagers held a dark opinion of the headmaster of Ponsonby Hall, Ned proved to be quite a charming gossip. He told me of the locked room. I think the time has come for Carruthers Minor to have the benefit of a second medical opinion. Are you up to a bit of house breaking, Watson?"

"You know I am."

"This is dangerous business. Bring your pistol. We'll also require a lantern. I have a job for you too, Lord Landers."

"I'm game for anything if it results in that evil man going to the gallows. What do you want me to do?"

"I need you to pay a call on Dr. Ponsonby this evening. Your purpose is to express your gratitude for his efforts to save the life of your brother by offering to endow his school to the tune of several thousand pounds. Insist that Mrs. Arkwright be present so you may reward her with a sum of money. While you keep them engaged, Watson and I will make our way to the first floor with a ladder that I observed when I was in the stable. I had pre-ferred to wait for the reply to my telegram to Jonas Appleby, but Watson's report on the boy in the locked room makes it neces-sary for us visit Ponsonby Hall without further delay."

With Lord Landers at the reins of a rented carriage, we arrived in the glow of fading dusk at the gate of a lengthy driveway leading to Ponsonby Hall. While he drove slowly to the bleak structure, Holmes and I made our way to the stables. As we neared it, I said, "Suppose that the handyman is inside."

"Don't worry about Ned," Holmes whispered. "Observing signs that he's a hard drinker, I thanked him for his employment advice by giving him a pint flask of whiskey."

"You think of everything!"

With the sky rapidly darkening and the ladder placed below a window toward the rear of the Hall, Holmes and I quickly ascended to the first floor and through the window into a dark corridor. Opening the shutter of the lantern, I directed a narrow shaft of light toward the end of the hallway and settled the beam on a door with a large padlock. Examining the lock closely, Holmes whispered, "It's a Folsom. As my old friend and expert cracksman Charlie Peace would attest if he hadn't been hanged in Armley Prison a decade ago, a Folsom is as easy to crack as a hard-boiled egg."

As we entered a pitch black room no larger than a prison cell, the terrified boy begged, "Please don't kill me, sir. I won't tell anybody, Dr. Ponsonby. Please don't let that thing get me."

"We're here to help you, lad," said I. Shining the light on him, I saw that he was lashed flat on his back to a narrow wooden bench with shacked legs downward and his bare feet on the floor. "You have nothing to fear now. This is the famous detective Sherlock Holmes."

While Holmes released him, the boy exclaimed, "Be careful you don't step on that thing. It's in here somewhere. Mrs. Arkwright let it loose."

"What thing?" I demanded.

"It's terrible creature that bites," the boy sobbed, "and don't let go!"

Sweeping the cubicle with the light of the lantern, I saw what appeared to be a large type of reptile in a corner. Flicking a hideous tongue from a gaping mouth with short ugly fangs, it hissed as it gazed at me angrily. Stepping toward it, I drew my revolver.

"Don't fire, Watson," Holmes exclaimed. "The shot will be heard downstairs."

Taking the gun from me, he maneuvered close to the animal. As it lunged toward him, he brought the butt of the pistol down hard twice on its thorny-looking back and proceeded to bash its monstrous head again and again and again.

Peering down at its battered and bloody remains, I asked. "What on earth is it?"

"There's no time for that now," he replied. Turning to the boy, he asked, "Lad. are you feeling well enough to assist us?"

"Yes, sir. I'm not sick and never was."

"Brave boy. Now go with Dr. Watson. There's a ladder at the window. I want you to hurry into the village and find the constable. Here is my card. Give it to the constable, and tell him I need him here as quickly as possible. You needn't worry about Dr. Ponsonby and Mrs. Arkwright. You'll never see them again."

Having seen Carruthers Minor down the ladder and scurrying off on his mission, I asked Holmes, "How can you say that he'll never see those people again? We have no evidence."

"I intend to frighten them into confessing to multiple murders of children."

My notes and published accounts of Sherlock Holmes confronting criminals with the fact that he had proved to be their undoing contained colorful descriptions of their reactions by words and facial expressions, but none of them had exhibited the look of astonishment and anxiety of Dr. Ponsonby when Holmes burst into the library with my revolver in his grip and declared, "The game is over. All that is needed is your admission of your guilt before Lord Landers, Dr. Watson, and myself to place both of you in the prisoner's dock and on the gallows."

"Your requirement of a confession, Holmes," replied Ponsonby with smug arrogance, "is an admission that you have no scintilla of proof against me."

"Wrong," I exclaimed, "We shall have the testimony of Carruthers Minor."

"The imaginings of an hysterical boy!"

"We also have the animal that was your means of murder," said Holmes.

"An animal, if that's what you claim to have, was brought here by you, no doubt in the service of Lord Landers on the basis of his ridiculous idea that his brother's death was not from the cause noted on the death certificate. He is obviously paying you handsomely to frame me."

"That," retorted Lord Landers, "is a filthy lie."

"As to the animal," said Holmes, "it is alive and in the room where you'd kept Carruthers Minor in the expectation that the creature would eventually bite him."

"I've had enough of this charade. I know nothing about this animal. Leave here at once."

Stepping boldly forward with the pistol pointed at Ponsonby, Holmes said, "Take off your shoes and stockings. Both of you! I intend to lock you in that room upstairs until you either confess or reap the death that you cruelly imposed on children. I understand the Gila Monster not only has an acute sense of smell for prey, but that the animal is ferocious if stepped on."

"For God's sake, Arthur," exclaimed Mrs. Arkwright with a terrified tone, "admit what this man obviously knows. Tell him everything."

"Shut up, woman! He's bluffing."

"That is a dangerous assumption," said Holmes. "Either confess now, or find yourself in the death chamber upstairs."

"It was his idea," the matron blurted. "He sent me to Arizona to get that awful reptile."

"It is established in English law," said Lord Landers, "that whoever assists in any way in the commission of murder or any other crime is equally guilty, madam. However, a person who aids in the prosecution of the primary figure in such a conspiracy can hope for leniency."

"I don't want to hang" the matron blurted. "He's the one who did all of it."

"You may consider yourself fortunate," I interjected, "that the animal didn't bite you as you brought it to England and when you turned it loose in the infirmary."

"On your word as a gentleman, Mr. Holmes, and Lord Landers' promise that you'll put in a good word for me," she pleaded, "I'll tell you and the police everything, and I'll stand up in court and repeat it."

"It will be your word against mine," retorted Ponsonby. "I will state that all of this was your doing. After all, it was you who brought the animal from America, not I."

"Yes, but I kept the detailed directions that you wrote out telling me who I was to see out there to get it. And you're the one who made out the false death certificates."

Stepping forward, Holmes said angrily, "I've had enough of this. The best way to settle this outrageous affair is to turn the matter over to the animal upstairs. Off with your shoes and stockings, Ponsonby."

Throwing up his hands, he exclaimed, "All right, all right. I admit everything."

"While we're waiting for the constable," said Holmes, "write out your confession. If it is not to my satisfaction, it's the room upstairs for you."

By the time Carruthers Minor returned with the constable, Ponsonby had completed a lengthy account of his crimes, including names of the despicable parents who had paid him to murder their sons. He explained that he had been inspired by reading my account of Grimesby Roylott's use of the Swamp Adder as a means of murder and decided to employ the poisonous reptile he had studied years earlier in a class on venoms while a medical student in Arizona.

After reading the document, Holmes said, "I also have a confession, Dr. Ponsonby. I *was* bluffing. Your devilish instrument of murder lies dead in the room above."

Upon our return to the inn, Holmes was presented with the reply to his telegram. "It is late in arriving, but confirms what I suspected," he said, handing it to me. "Jonas Appleby is the leading expert on the fauna of the American West. He has written on the subject extensively, including a recent article that I read in a scientific journal devoted to poisonous reptiles dealing with the species *Heloderma*. Known as the Gila Monster, it is named for its domain in the Gila River valley in Arizona. When Llewellyn Coffin described the bite marks on the legs and arms of the victims, I recalled Ponsonby's medical training in Arizona and proceeded on the logical conclusion that he was using a Gila Monster."

The prosecutions that followed became the greatest scandal in the history of Wales. For Holmes's brilliant work in bringing to an end the singular case of the dying schoolboys, the Prince of Wales awarded him a specially struck medal that Holmes placed in a drawer of his desk where he kept souvenirs of some of his most challenging cases.

Lord Landers expressed his gratitude with a sum equal to more than three years of rental payments to Mrs. Hudson at an address that Holmes had made world-famous.

· 10 ·

The Adventure of the Sally Martin

On a sparkling Thursday afternoon in July of Queen Victoria's 1897 Jubilee Year, Sherlock Holmes returned from an unexplained sojourn somewhere in the city and immediately sat at his desk to examine the contents of the afternoon post.

"Hello," he said presently. "This is very interesting."

Engaged in examining my own meager and lackluster delivery of correspondence, I dared to joke, "What is it? Another damsel in distress? Crisis in Cornwall? Has there been a mysterious death in Derbyshire?"

"It's an invitation," he replied, bringing the letter to me. "What are you able to deduce?"

The stationery was that of the firm of George Byron, the Lancashire cotton manufacturer, art and antiques collector, and flagrant flaunter of his enormous wealth. Noting that it had been signed in an ostentatious manner, I responded, "He thinks quite highly of himself."

"A great deal of money often has that effect on some men who started life with nothing and clawed their way to the top," Holmes replied as he sank into his favorite chair. "Handwriting can be a window into one's entire life and an indicator of character. What of the content?"

The letter read:

My dear Mr. Holmes,

To apprize you of a personal matter of the utmost urgency and moment and elicit your advice, I request the honor of your presence on the morning of Wednesday next for the christening of my yacht *Sally Martin* in the town of Kingsgate. Arrangements will be made for your accommodation at the Silver Dolphin Inn.

Most sincerely,
George Byron

"Except for the part about the yacht, it seems no different from countless communications that you receive soliciting your services."

"Once again, Watson, you have missed the point. Two points, actually. If the matter is so urgent why did he send a letter, rather than a telegram? If it is of such moment, why the delay in conferring with me for six days?"

"He probably assumed that stressing urgency was the only certain way of gaining your attention and assuring himself that you would come to Kingsgate."

"What caught my attention was not the language he used, but that fact that the letter was not dictated to a secretary and done on a typewriter."

"Shall I deduce from this that you intend to accept his invitation?"

"Only on the condition that the accommodation at the inn is for two. You've looked a little worldweary of late. You could use a couple of days at the seaside."

"Do you know that I have never been on a yacht?"

"According to Lloyd's of London, cited in a recent article in the *Times*, the *Sally Martin* is a yacht that surpasses all others in terms of dimensions and luxurious appointments, including Her Majesty's. Whether it will rank as highly in interest to me as the vessel in my first case, the *Gloria Scott*, or even the *Friesland* of dubious memory, remains to be seen."

I had learned about the former transport ship many years after Holmes's involvement in the case while he was a student at university. Although *Gloria Scott* was entered on the registry as a passenger ship that foundered and was lost at sea, she had been carrying several convicts to Australia and was taken over by them in a bloody revolt. This event led ultimately to a murder that became Holmes's first venture into criminal investigation. The *Friesland* was a Dutch steamship at the heart of an adventure that nearly cost us our lives, but the matter was of such a shocking and sensitive nature that Holmes would not permit me to reveal it. My notes were therefore consigned with other secrets in a tin dispatch box that I keep in a vault of Cox & Co. in Charing Cross Road. Other memorable ships' names in my files of Holmes's cases include the *Esmeralda, Matilda Briggs, Rock of Gibraltar, Ruritania, Orontes, Palmyra, Norah Creina, Alicia,* and the river steam launch *Aurora*. In contrast to Holmes's interest in maritime matters, my experience with seas and the hardy men who plied them was reading Clark Russell's fine sea stories, Robert Louis Stevenson, and the American writer Herman Melville.

My papers also record Holmes's affinity for those who go down to the sea. Perhaps the most notable of these was Captain Jack Croker, whom Holmes allowed to flee the country after Croker killed the despicably brutal wife abuser Sir Eustace Brackenstall. This fascination with the ways and unique habits of mariners led to a study of tattoos and a monograph on variations of design and execution of skin adornments. These were categorized by individual practitioners of the art and their unique styles, varieties of subjects, colors and types of ink, characteristics of needles, and singularities, which indicated when and where in the world the tattoos were likely to have been applied. This accumulation of data invariably produced surprise and bewilderment in men who encountered Sherlock Holmes for the first time and found themselves subjected to his discourse on the tattoos they wore on hands, wrists, arms, and occasionally on their faces.

In the instance of an old salt who walked up to our table in the Silver Dolphin Inn dining room on the evening of our arrival in the small fishing town on the Kentish coast, the large tattoo upon his left wrist was a depiction of a sailor poised to attack a shark with a knife.

"I know who you are," he exclaimed loudly as he approached. "Sherlock Holmes is who. I know you on account of you put my brother Alf in prison a few years ago on a charge of blackmail. Well, I've been waitin' a long time for this moment."

With an amused smile, Holmes replied, "Now that it's come, what do you intend to do?"

"Don't worry, Mr. Holmes," he said, helping himself to a

chair. "All I want to do is thank you. By puttin' Alf away, you cleared it for me to take up with his wife. I'd like to stand you and your friend to some ale. My name is Albert Jones."

As the man signaled for a waiter, Holmes glanced at his forearm and asked, "How many years did you spend at sea in the Singapore Strait?"

"Seven. Say, how did you know—?"

"Your tattoo could have been done only in a tattoo parlor across from the Raffles Hotel. The design is unusual, however."

"One of a kind! It shows the fight I had with the biggest Great White you ever saw."

With the delivery of three pints of ale, Jones launched a tale of a struggle against the shark in the aftermath of a typhoon that had cast him overboard with only a pocketknife. As he spun the yarn, he revealed a gift for story-telling that rivaled anything that I had read from the pens of Russell, Melville and Stevenson. How much of it was true and what portions had been embroidered through the years of retelling became irrelevant.

As he related the bloody climax of the tale, I observed Holmes peering toward the door to the dining room. "It seems, Watson," he said, "that the police have arrived."

Turning to see what he meant, I saw a stout, middleaged man in a black derby hat and the type of brown tweed suit that seemed to be a police standard issue everywhere. He was in a conversation with the waiter who had served our drinks. When the server pointed a finger in our direction, the obvious detective strode to our table with a grim expression. "Excuse me for this intrusion, Mr. Holmes," he said. "I'm Sergeant Dobson of the Kingsgate police. I heard you were in town for the christening of the *Sally Martin,* and I'm glad of it."

"What's the problem?" I asked.

"There's been a murder, and this sort of thing is not what we're accustomed to handling in these parts. My last case was more than fifteen years ago, and the culprit confessed."

"I'm at your service, Sergeant," said Holmes. "Who's been murdered?"

"Brace yourself, gentlemen. The victim is your host, Mr. George Byron. He was found stabbed to death in his cabin. I've left a constable on the boat and sent for the Canterbury police, but they can't be here until the morning. Remembering that you were on the list of guests for the christening that Mr. Byron gave me, I was hoping that you could have this all wrapped up by the time the Canterbury detectives arrive. I've got another constable waiting for us with a rowboat. I was also hoping that Dr. Watson would have a look at Mrs. Byron. She was acting hysterically, and I thought she might need something to quiet her down. Can you help along that line, sir?"

"I never travel without my physician's bag."

Leaving Albert Jones with a fresh pint of ale, and after a few minutes for me to collect my bag, we departed the inn. "Did you think it was curious, Sergeant Dobson," Holmes inquired as we walked briskly to the dock, "that Byron felt it necessary to give you a list of the people he'd invited to the christening?"

"I took it as a courtesy."

"How many of the people on the list are on the yacht at the moment?"

"Most guests aren't expected in town until tomorrow. There are three aboard right now and two crewmen, if you call the captain a member of the crew."

"Only two crew on such a large ship?"

"The captain says the rest are supposed to report on board in the morning. Mrs. Byron is there, along with Byron's brother Clarence and Joseph Hartson, the private secretary."

"What can you tell me about them?"

"Mrs. Byron is a lot younger than him. A bit on the flighty side. She was having a proper fit of hysterics. Clarence Byron was as cool as a cucumber. Hartson seemed a gentleman, but I got the feeling that Mrs. Byron has quite an eye for him. Maybe that's the policeman in me."

"The crew members?"

"There's Captain Jeremy Small and the deck hand, Arthur Coggins. A surly bloke! He gave me quite a bit of back talk when I questioned him. He's known to the police."

"Why?"

"The charges were minor. Petty theft, vagrancy, pub brawl. He's got a fiery temper. It may be on account of him working in carnivals between stints at sea."

Although a thin fog enveloped Kingsgate as we arrived at the dock and climbed into the rowboat, we could see the lights of the yacht. Anchored about a quarter of a mile distant, *Sally Martin* was a long, graceful two-masted ship with furled sails. Noting a carved figure of a half-nude woman on the sharp prow, I commented, "That's quite a risqué figurehead."

"The scuttlebutt among the town's sailors," said Dobson as we reached a ladder at the side of the royal blue, gold-trimmed boat, "is that Mr. Byron named the yacht after a young woman he had an affair with some years ago, before he went into the cotton business, made a fortune, and got married to a woman half his age. Whether there really was a girl named Sally Martin in his past I have no way of knowing. I like to think there was."

With a chuckle, Holmes asked, "Is that the married man in you speaking?"

"Very droll, Mr. Holmes."

"Where was the body found?"

"In Mr. Byron's cabin. You'll find everything just the way I did. It's a gruesome picture, but probably nothing you and Dr. Watson haven't seen many times."

"With the exception of manual strangulation," Holmes replied as we reached the cabin, "a blade is not only the most intimate of murder weapons, but an assurance that the deed will be done without attracting attention."

The corpse lay on its back in pajamas in the middle of the bed with a knife sunk into the center of his chest to the hilt. "To drive it that deeply," I ventured, "would require a great deal of force. The killer is obviously a man."

"Or an angry woman," Holmes replied as he studied the knife's large grip. "The delicate carving of the handle suggests the work of the indigenous population of the Andaman Islands. You recall, I'm sure, Watson, that the late Major John Sholto had several similar knives which he acquired during his service in India. This specimen, however, is much too undistinguished to have appealed to Mr. Byron's discriminating taste in collecting folk art. Aside from the knife, Watson, what does the tableau in this cabin reveal of the circumstances of this murder?"

"It's a simple story," I answered as I placed my bag on a chair. "Somebody opened the door, came in, surprised Mr. Byron, and stabbed him."

"What was Byron doing?"

"He was lying in bed."

"There's an open book in his right hand. This and the fact

that the bed coverings have not been disturbed eliminate both surprise and a struggle against his assailant. Byron simply kept on reading his book until the blow was struck."

"Therefore, whoever did this was someone who could come in upon him at will. There are three such persons on board. His wife, the brother, and the secretary."

"Four persons, Watson. I'm confident that Captain Small could also take that liberty."

"In my limited experience with cases where the husband is the victim," said Dobson, "the person to talk to first is the wife. And the husband if it's the wife who's dead. As I said, I think she has eyes for the handsome secretary. She also stands to inherit a fortune."

"Excellent motives, indeed, Sergeant," I replied, "but you told us that the woman was hysterical after she learned of the death of her husband."

"Did you never hear of crocodile tears, Doctor?"

"The Dobson rule of suspecting the spouse is a sound one," said Holmes. "Shall we see if Mrs. Byron is sufficiently recovered to answer a few questions? She may be able to shed light on persons who might have other motives for murdering George Byron."

A young blonde with tear-streaked face and reddened eyes from crying, Mrs. Byron glared defiantly when we entered the cabin. She demanded, "What is this then, Sergeant? You said the other police wouldn't be here till morning. Who are these men?"

"This is Sherlock Holmes and Dr. John H. Watson. I've requested their assistance. If you wish, Dr. Watson can administer a sedative."

With a sob and blotting tears with the corner of a lace handkerchief, she said, "I don't need no sedative, and I'm not interested in being interrogated by Sherlock Holmes. I fail to see how this is any of their business."

"It became my business," Holmes said sharply, "when your husband engaged me on the matter of a personal nature."

With an expression of shock, she asked, "When did George do that?"

Dobson declared, "Just answer Mr. Holmes's questions."

Emitting another sob, Mrs. Byron asked, "How can you think that I did this, Sergeant?"

"Everyone on this boat is a suspect until cleared," Dobson replied. "And there is the fact, as you told me when I first questioned you, that you are in Mr. Byron's will for everything."

Glancing around the small cabin, Holmes asked, "Can you suggest anyone who might have had a reason to kill your husband?"

"Plenty. George was a hard businessman. He made lots of enemies."

"None of whom were on board tonight."

"No, but his brother is."

"Are you proposing," I inquired, "that Clarence Byron did this?"

"There's a dark side of Clarence that people don't see. George certainly didn't. He just let Clarence go on sponging off him despite my complaining that Clarence had made improper advances in my direction several times. It's also true that Clarence didn't take kindly to him not being in the will anymore. He took it hard when George told him everything would go to me."

"Thank you, Mrs. Byron," said Holmes. "You have my and Dr. Watson's condolences."

Upon our leaving the cabin, Dobson said, "Clarence Byron's cabin is down at the end of the corridor, Mr. Holmes."

"Where is the secretary's?"

"Downstairs where the crew stays."

"Secretaries can be valuable sources of information."

A fine-looking young man wearing a Masonic pin in the lapel of a well-tailored suit and a crisp white shirt with gold cuff links to match a handsome watch chain and a small signet ring, Joseph Hartson responded to being introduced to Sherlock Holmes as cordially as the wife had been hostile. "I was surprised to find your name on the guest list for the christening, Mr. Holmes," he said amicably, "and how fortunate it is for the police that it was."

"Thank you. When as the last time you saw your employer?"

"Shortly after dinner. He was taking a turn around the deck. That was around a quarter to ten. I went directly to bed. I was awakened by Sergeant Dobson with the horrible news."

"Did Mr. Byron sometimes handle his correspondence without your assistance?"

"If he did so, how would I know? I would be surprised, however. I am—that is, was—his confidential secretary. He consigned almost everything to me and relied on me to inform him of matters I considered beyond my province."

"Can you share an example?"

"The latest instance concerned his brother. I had the unpleasant occasion yesterday to inform Mr. Byron that I believed Clarence had forged Mr. Byron's signature on a bank draft for five hundred pounds. The brothers had a terrible row about it."

"My next question may seem indelicate, but I must pose it."

"Ask anything you wish, Mr. Holmes."

"What is your relationship to Mrs. Byron?"

"She has been very kind to me. My family are dead, and

she's taken an interest in me, but I give you my word as a gentleman that it's been purely platonic."

"Thank you. I may have further questions."

"I'm not a policeman, sir, but in my opinion, Clarence is the one who did this."

On the way to Clarence Byron's cabin, I remarked, "The finger of guilt certainly points to the brother."

"So we are being led to believe," Holmes replied.

As Dobson knocked on the door of the cabin, a voice within shouted, "Help me!"

Barging in, the sergeant demanded, "What's the trouble?"

Flat on his back on the bed, Clarence Brown clutched at his chest and said, "I fear I'm having a heart attack. I need a doctor. Send for one immediately."

Striding to him, I replied, "It so happens that I am a physician."

"Really? Where's your bag?"

After checking the pulse in his right wrist, I placed my ear to his chest and replied, "I left my bag in Mr. Byron's cabin. Now please be quiet."

"Well, hurry and fetch he bag, man! I could be dying."

"Nonsense," I exclaimed as I drew back. "You're as healthy as I am."

"You're not a doctor. You're a charlatan."

"If you were having a heart attack, your heartbeat would not be normal, as it definitely is. You would be sweating profusely, your skin would feel clammy, you would have difficulty breathing, and you certainly would not be able to order people around. You're the charlatan, sir!"

"All right, all right. I was shamming, but only because I was afraid you'd come here to arrest me on a charge of killing my brother. I have no doubt that's what my sister-in-law wants."

"Whether I charge you with murder remains to be seen," replied Dobson, "but you can count your lucky stars your brother didn't bring a charge of larceny by forgery against you."

"I have no idea what you're talking about."

"I refer to your forgery of your brother's signature on a bank draft to acquire the sum of five hundred pounds."

Byron suddenly sat up and declared, "Retract that statement, sir. It is a confounded lie. I demand to know who told you that calumny."

"Where and how I learned of it and from whom is police business."

"As long as accusations are being made, I'll make one myself. You'd do well to look at the deck hand Coggins. Just a few days ago, I heard him threatening George."

"How very convenient."

"It's the truth. I came upon the two of them having an argument on deck."

"What was the substance of the argument?"

"Coggins was complaining about how he's been treated. He apparently took offense at my brother not knowing his name. I distinctly remember Coggins objecting to George's way of addressing him as 'you there,' 'boy,' and 'whatever your name is.' My brother could be that way. Unfeeling. Inconsiderate in the extreme. Dismissive of anyone he considered below him. But that's not my only reason for thinking Coggins killed George. After the argument, he said to me that one day he'd see that my brother would get what was coming to him. Did you know that Coggins is an expert knife thrower? He made part of his living doing it as a carnival performer. If you don't believe me, you can ask Captain Small about him."

Tall and trim in a smart uniform and with short salt and

pepper hair and Van Dyke beard, the master of the *Sally Martin* might have posed for a John Singer Sargent portrait of the type of men who had made it possible for Britannia to rule the waves. Welcoming us into his quarters, he opened the conversation with a tone of combined sadness and exasperation. "This is a tragic day," he said. "It's not how I expected to launch my retirement as an admiral of Her Majesty's fleet. Rather than a joyous christening of as fine a yacht I've ever set foot on, I'm faced with the necessity of carrying out Mr. Byron's request for a burial at sea."

"When did he express this desire?" asked Holmes.

"He told me last week. It set me back on my heels. Mr. Byron was not that old, and he seemed to be fit as a fiddle."

"I understand that you signed up Arthur Coggins to be member of your crew."

"Never! Coggins is not the type of man I'd want on any ship of mine."

"Then who hired him?"

"Coggins said he'd been signed at the request of Mr. Byron."

This startling revelation suddenly became secondary when we heard a gunshot from the deck below. A moment later, Joseph Hartson burst into the captain's cabin shouting, "Sergeant Dobson, come quick. Coggins has killed himself!"

The body was on the floor in the center of the tiny cabin with a bullet wound behind the right ear. A still-smoking revolver lay loosely in his right hand. A small piece of paper taken by Holmes from the left read:

I killed him. With my record I knew you'd catch me, so
I took the quick and easy way out.

"Suicide and a confession," said Dobson. "The case is solved, Holmes."

"Far from it, Sergeant. If you examine his hands, you'll find more calluses on the left than the other. Why and how does a lefthanded man shoot himself with a gun in the right? You will also find that the note was not written by a lefthanded person."

Looking as pale as a ghost, Captain Small muttered, "Lord save me, this is a death ship."

"You said, Captain, that you didn't hire Coggins. Where might the person who did have gone to engage him?"

"Most able seamen who are looking to sign on a ship in these parts put their names on a registry at the Seamen's Hostel. When a man gets a job, the name of person who signs him up and the name of the ship are recorded in a ledger. The hostel is next to the Red Lion pub on the wharf. The owner is old Meyer Jenkins, but it's run by his harridan of a wife."

Dobson's description and warning proved accurate. In the course of my association with Holmes, I had never encountered so disagreeable and profane a woman as the one who opened the door of the hostel shortly after midnight. Short, stout, middle-aged, she reeked of the odor of whiskey. A foul-smelling, cheap, black cigarillo jutted from the left corner of her mouth. She greeted us with a hard look and declared, "This is a fine time of the night to root a respectable woman out of a warm bed, even if you two are a pair of swells. What the devil do you want?"

"We apologize for the intrusion at such late hour, madam," said Holmes. "We require your assistance in solving two murders."

"So that's it. You're the police. Well, I don't know nothing about any murders."

"One of the victims," said Holmes, "was Arthur Coggins."

The woman gasped and stepped back. "Arthur was murdered? Who by?"

"Our hope is that you can help identify the murderer. I have reason to believe Coggins was killed by the person who hired him to work on the yacht *Sally Martin*."

"How do expect me to know that?"

"His name is in the hiring ledger."

"Oh that. Come in, and I'll get it for you. It's too bad about Arthur, but I can't say that I'm surprised he came to a bad end. He had a devil of a temper and was always quick to pull out a knife to settle things. Two years ago on his last ship, he got mixed up in a knife fight and got arrested, but the police couldn't make a murder charge stick. Since then, poor Arthur couldn't get another berth on account of captains not wanting to risk trouble. I was very happy for him on the day that the gentleman signed him up."

"Then you do remember who hired Coggins," said I.

"I said I didn't know the name, but I recall the man because I admired his good taste in jewelry. I had no reason to ask his name since he was required to write it in the ledger." Giving the book to Holmes, she continued, "All the information is on the last page."

The signature under the listing for employer was that of Clarence Byron. "I knew it," I muttered. "I felt in my bones that he had to be our man."

Turning to the surly proprietress, Holmes said, "My good woman, it will be necessary for me to borrow this ledger."

"Here now, that's a bit irregular."

"You can allow me to take it, or hand it over to the police. In either instance, it will be returned in a few hours."

"Go ahead and take it. I've lost enough sleep."

Walking to the rowboat that would take us back to the *Sally*

Martin, I ventured, "It's a rarity when a criminal signs his name to this crime."

With a nod of greeting to the constable who would man the boat, Holmes replied, "This signature doesn't amount to proof of murder."

"Everything points to his guilt," said I as we got into the boat. "It's clear that Clarence was attempting to lay the murder of Byron at Coggins's feet by concocting the story about him observing Coggins and Byron having an argument. He'd engaged the man because he knew of his criminal record. He killed his brother with a knife, then murdered Coggins, and made it look as if it were suicide by putting the pistol in Coggins' right hand and leaving the note. His mistake was not knowing he was lefthanded."

"Your analysis is logical, Watson, but you have overlooked one important fact that did not go unnoticed by the observant operator of this hostel."

"What fact would that be?"

"I call your attention to her reference to the taste in jewelry of the man who signed his name in this ledger. The key to unlocking this mystery is the signature. As I stated at the start of this singular adventure, you can learn much by studying handwriting. I hope that by testing my theory, we shall identify a double murderer."

"How do you plan to accomplish that?"

"By asking Sergeant Dobson to order the four people who were aboard the *Sally Martin* at the time of these murders to provide samples of their handwriting."

"Surely, you don't suspect Captain Small?"

"Give me a reason why I shouldn't."

"Great scot! He's a former admiral of the fleet!"

"Accepting Her Majesty's shilling and donning an army or

naval uniform does not place a man above suspicion, Watson. Before Sebastian Moran threw in with Professor Moriarty, he was a colonel in the Indian Army."

"The Indian Army," I retorted, "not the Regular Army."

Within minutes of our return to the yacht, Sergeant Dobson assembled Mrs. Byron, her brother-in-law, Joseph Hartson, and Captain Small in the ship's large lounge. When they were seated, Holmes presented each with a writing pad and pencil, and explained, "I have given you these writing implements for the purpose of taking down by dictation a letter that I recently received from George Byron. When you are finished, sign your names, please."

Clarence Byron demanded, "What letter?"

"This is nonsense, " said Hartson. "If there were such a letter, I would have known of it."

"You didn't know of it because George Byron wrote it himself."

Sergeant Dobson stepped forward and demanded, "All of you do what Mr. Holmes wants, or your refusal will be officially noted."

Drawing the letter from a pocket, Holmes said, "It's a short note."

Upon completion of Holmes's reading of the missive slowly enough for the words to be taken down, Dobson collected the writing pads and presented them to him. "I'm sure you know what you're doing, Mr. Holmes," he whispered, "but I can't see what you're up to."

Thereupon, a silence descended upon the lounge. Everyone's eyes were fixed on Holmes as he examined the four samples of handwriting. After several tense minutes, he said, "Sergeant Dobson, I recommend that you arrest Joseph Hartson on suspicion of murdering his employer and the deck hand Coggins."

Bounding to his feet, Hartson exclaimed, "This is outrageous."

"When the time comes," said Holmes quietly, "I will testify that the fabricated suicide note found in Coggins's hand was written by you, as was the forged signature of Clarence Byron in the ledger recording the hiring of Coggins to be a member of the *Sally Martin* crew. There is no question that the letters 'r' in the faked suicide note, the signature in the ledger and at the bottom of the letter I dictated were written by you. I can point out several other characteristics, including slanting of the letters, thickness of stokes, and formation of capitals. If my testimony is deemed insufficient to persuade a jury of your guilt in the murder of Coggins, which was vital to your scheme to murder George Byron, your fingerprints on the page of the ledger will connect you to the hiring of Coggins, as well as to the forgery of Clarence Byron's name. The woman who runs the Seamen's Hostel will also attest to admiring your jewelry on the day you posed as Clarence Byron to hire Coggins."

"This is balderdash," railed Hartson. "I had no reason to kill George Byron."

"You had compelling reasons. The first was to avoid a charge of embezzlement, which I believe was the motivation for Mr. Byron writing to me for advice on a personal matter in a note he took pains to keep secret from his private secretary. When I questioned you in your cabin, you volunteered the story about Clarence Byron's forgery and the argument between the brothers. You also had a desire to be rid of George Byron so you could ultimately marry his widow. This and the prospect of an enormous inheritance was why she joined your conspiracy."

"That is ridiculous," objected Mrs. Byron.

"To ensure that your inheritance would not be challenged in court by Clarence Byron," Holmes replied, "he also had to be eliminated through the device of creating a phony story about

Clarence being a forger and Hartson's tale about his clashing with his brother about it. There is no point in denying it. Your lover will certainly be convicted on the basis of his writing and his fingerprints, along with Mrs. Jenkins's identification, an eventuality which I doubt he is willing to accept alone."

Collapsing back into his chair with a groan, Hartson answered, "You're right about that, Holmes. The crazy part is, this was all her idea. I'll testify to that."

"What you mean," said Mrs. Byron, "is that you'll lie about it."

"Whether he testifies or not," interjected Sergeant Dobson, "detectives from Canterbury have a way of getting what they want out of people they arrest for murder. You can avoid that unpleasantness, Mrs. Byron, by admitting everything to me, with Mr. Holmes, Dr. Watson, and the captain as witnesses. That way, when the Canterbury boys arrive, I'll be able to inform them the case is solved and send them on their way."

Emitting a long sigh, she glared for a moment at Holmes and broke down in tears. "I can see that the game is up. I'll tell you everything."

"I'm afraid telling us won't be enough," said Dobson with a satisfied glance at Holmes. "I'll require confessions from both of you . . . *in writing*."

· 11 ·

The Adventure of the Grand Old Man

On a Tuesday afternoon at the height of the London theatrical season between May and July, I was looking forward to returning to a gossipy biography of William
Gladstone. My immersion in the book had been interrupted for
more than week while I assisted Sherlock Holmes in dealing with
a scandal at the Nonpareil Club. I had barely resumed and
reached a very amusing passage in which Queen Victoria complained that the prime minister spoke to her as if she were a public
meeting when Holmes shattered the silence of the sitting room.

"What could be better, Watson, than a ticket to a great play?"

"Being able to read without disruption."

"Two tickets! These in my hand are for box seats at the
revival of the finest drama of our era, *The Road Is Narrow*. It
opens on Friday night. They are compliments of the manager

of the Imperial Theater at the request of the playwright, Martin Reeve. When you and I saw the play some ten tears ago, it was in its third year of production and sold out for the next season. The leading role in this mounting is the great tragedian Sir Basil Wentworth."

"He may be a superb actor and you may consider *The Road Is Narrow* the finest drama since Shakespeare, but I recall falling asleep from boredom."

"Does that mean you are not interested in using the second ticket?"

Laying aside the book, I answered, "I wouldn't miss this outing for the world, but not because of either the play or the actor. I'll go because it's apparent that you were not given the tickets in a burst of generosity on the part of Mr. Reeve. He obviously wants you to undertake something for him."

"Very good, old friend! You are developing the deductive skills of a first-rate detective."

"What puzzles me is why he doesn't call on you here."

"It's been my experience that successful playwrights invariably choose the most dramatic setting to conduct even the most routine and trivial activities. They are always making grand entrances or insinuating their names into the newspapers and magazines. Living proof of this is Mr. Oscar Wilde. He has become famous, or notorious if you prefer, for his performances in public places in order to garner publicity. Martin Reeve engaged in such exhibitionism when he married the only daughter of Lord Selfridge two years after his triumph. The wedding ring contained the famous Carstairs diamond. When his wife died three years after the birth of their only child, he inherited her fortune and withdrew from the limelight by residing as a recluse near Carlisle. He wrote a few plays that fell far short artistically of *The Road Is Narrow*. As he has been a hermit for nearly thirty years, I believe the Grand Old Man of the West End has selected a theater for the consultation with me either because it is either a convenience for a man of his advanced age, or he feels that he does not wish to be observed making a visit to Baker Street. We shall learn which on Friday."

Perhaps because Sherlock Holmes believed he could have been a great thespian had he not discovered and honed his unique talent for the solving of crimes, he had always felt a need to end a case with a flourish of theatricality. What intrigued me was his recognition of this.

"Some touch of the artist wells up within me," he confessed in the investigation into the so-called Hound of the Baskervilles, "and calls insistently for a well-staged performance."

On yet another occasion, he admitted, "It is not really difficult to construct a series of inferences, each dependent upon its predecessor, and each simple in itself. If, after doing so, one simply knocks out all the central inferences and presents one's audience with the starting point and conclusion, one may produce a startling effect."

Love of the theater was rivaled by his fascination with music and musicians. This may have been because he felt he could have been a renowned violinist. During our association, I was frequently commanded to abandon whatever I planned for an evening to attend a concert. The most memorable of these occasions occurred while he was deeply engaged in the matter of the Red Headed League. Informing me that the Spanish violinist and composer Sarasate would be performing that day, he insisted I accompany him to St. James's Hall, leaving the mystery of Jabez Wilson's employment to copy out the Encyclopedia Britannica for later.

Having made up his mind to use the theater tickets, he immediately shifted his attention to the consideration of other matters. With no case to pursue, he spent most of the time until Friday either conducting chemical experiments or catching up on filing documents, notes, and other ephemera that had accumulated into seemingly haphazard stacks in almost every part of the room. "Touch nothing," he warned our exasperated landlady. "Weighty issues depend on this material being where I can readily lay my hands on it."

The prospect of an evening at the theater and the likelihood of being presented with a problem to be resolved combined to lift Holmes's spirit more than the wine that accompanied a light meal partaken at Restivo's in Haymarket Square. As always when we dined out, we were seated at a table by the front window, allowing Holmes to keenly observe the tableau of the restless street beyond.

"What a fascinating mixture of humanity one finds sur-rounding a theater in the hour before the curtain rises," he said as he gazed at the throng. "Impeccably attired gentlemen and their ladies, the buskers providing their unique street perform-ances, Scotland Yarders looking out for pickpockets. They wear plainclothes, but to a dip they are as conspicuous as a Bobby in uniform and beehive helmet. And there are the people passing by who have better uses for their hard-earned wages than spending them for seats in a theater. I must say, this opening night has drawn a very large number of those for whom money is never a consideration."

"That may be due to the fact that the publication by the Palace in the *Times* of the Prince of Wales' schedule indicated that His Highness will be attending tonight's performance."

"With the Princess Alexandra, I wonder, or with one of his

innumerable mistresses chosen from the city's bevy of professional beauties?"

"You can be such a gossip, Holmes."

"Prince Edward should be more discreet. I hope he arrives on time. Nothing is ruder than keeping an audience waiting until royalty has been seated. Finish your glass of wine, Watson. The game is afoot."

Fortunately, the Prince of Wales, accompanied by his radiant wife, arrived two minutes before the play was to commence. But as the audience's applause for the royal couple subsided and the gold curtain rose, the only occupants in our box were Holmes and myself. At the end of the first act of the drama that I found as tedious and dense as it had seemed a decade before, we were still by ourselves. When the playwright had not appeared by the second intermission, I was convinced that there had been a misunderstanding and that Mr. Reeve had not sent Holmes the tickets as a means of consulting him discreetly. Having no desire to sit through the rest of the play, I was about to leave Holmes in solitary bliss, when a much younger gentleman than the playwright entered the box.

"Allow me to introduce myself and explain," he said, sitting next to Holmes. "I am the business manager for Mr. Reeve. I sent you the tickets. Mr. Reeve is quite ill and does not know that I made these arrangements. The only person who does is his physician, Harvey Manners. He asked me to arrange this meeting because he was unable to come himself. He is convinced that someone is trying to murder Mr. Reeve. He hopes, as do I, that you will go to Carlisle and investigate. If you agree to undertake this investigation, Dr. Manners will meet you tomorrow afternoon at the Carlisle railway station. There is a train from St. Pancras that leaves at eight in the morning."

With both the train and Dr. Manners on time, Holmes immediately required a report.

"I've been in almost daily attendance to Mr. Reeve," Manners began. "He suffers from hereditary cardiac arrhythmia. He's sixty-two years old, the age his father passed away from the same affliction, and the prognosis is not good. A severe shock would certainly bring on an attack that could be fatal. My fear is that whoever is trying to kill him is trying to provoke one."

"Details, Dr. Manners. I need details "

"Around ten o'clock last night, his coachman came to my residence to summon me. When I arrived at Mr. Reeve's house, he was in state of near hysteria. After I gave him a shot to calm him down, he claimed he'd seen an apparition."

"In what form?"

"He said it was a ghost from his past."

"Pardon me," I interjected. "If I may venture an opinion as a physician, this appears to me to be a manifestation of senile dementia. There have been several interesting studies of the phenomenon published in recent years."

"I'm familiar with the literature, but I believe that whatever Mr. Reeve saw was real and that it was arranged by whoever wants to see him dead."

"This is fantastic," I replied. "Who would want to kill a dying man?"

"The more pertinent question," said Holmes, "is who was in the house last night?"

"There are two servants who have been with him for decades and the three people who reside with Mr. Reeve, his daughter Catherine, his brother Silas, who is a drunkard and good for nothing, and Mr. Reeve's secretary, a young fellow named Hugh Kingslake."

"Do you know who benefits from Mr. Reeve's will?"

"I am familiar with the provisions of the previous will."

"He drew up a new one? When?"

"A few days ago he said he planned to draft a revision."

"Was Mr. Reeve able to describe the apparition?"

"The man was not completely coherent, but I gathered that this ghost from out of his past was a young man with blond hair and blue eyes. I thought at first that he was recalling someone he had known years ago, perhaps a classmate at school."

"What convinced you this blue-eyed youth might was not a figment of the imagination?"

"After I gave Mr. Reeve the sedative, I looked around his bedroom and found these on the window sill." Drawing an envelope from a pocket, Manners took from within it two strands of hair and handed them to Holmes. "You'll note that they are blond, but everyone in that house has brown hair."

Examining the strands, Holmes said, "These are human hair, but they are from a wig. See the minute particles of adhesive adhering to the roots? No ghost I know of wears a hairpiece. We must go to the house immediately."

"Please proceed carefully, Mr. Holmes. The old man was told that you were calling as an admirer of his work. I'd feel terrible if your presence as a detective provided the shock which killed my patient. As to your fee—"

"My charges are on a fixed scale. Have you told anyone about the hairs you found?"

"No."

"Excellent."

Set at the edge of a wood several miles from the town, the playwright's house was larger than I had expected. Considering the fact that Holmes had informed me that Martin Reeve had not repeated the huge success of his first play, I anticipated finding a modest cottage of the sort that Holmes frequently envisaged settling into when he decided to retire. We were greeted at the door by a young man. Introducing himself as Hugh Kingslake, he invited us into a spacious and opulent parlor. "I'm most relieved that you're here, Mr. Holmes," he said. "I do agree with Dr. Manners that someone deliberately induced the shock that Mr. Reeve suffered the other night."

"Do you suspect anyone in particular?"

Before the secretary could reply, the door to the parlor opened, and a man of middle age entered in an obvious state of agitation. Glaring at Kingslake, he demanded, "Who are these people, and what do they want?"

"Allow me to introduce Sherlock Holmes and Dr. John H. Watson."

"Sherlock Holmes, eh? Well, we have no need of a professional meddler."

With a slight smile, Holmes asked, "And you, sir, are?"

"Silas Reeve. I will not allow you to upset my brother. Who is responsible for this bloody intrusion? No, don't tell me. It was the busybody Dr. Manners. I told him when I saw him on the stairs as he was going up to see Martin, and I'm telling you, that this business of Martin seeing a ghost is stuff and nonsense. I can imagine what Manners has been telling you, that I'm the black sheep of the family and a drunkard who's been sponging off my brother. Well, what goes on in this family isn't his concern, and it isn't yours either."

"Sir, I have traveled some two hundred miles to see your brother, and I intend to do so."

At this heated moment, a young woman entered the parlor and exclaimed, "Uncle Silas, hold your tongue!"

"Ah the loving daughter Catherine. She is no doubt going to order her drunken old uncle to go to his room. Don't be deceived by what she says, Mr. Holmes. The lady is not as caring about her father as she pretends. It's no secret that I've been living off my brother, but it's also not a secret that dear Catherine is looking forward to all the money she's in line to inherit, so she can share it with my brother's supposedly devoted secretary."

"Uncle Silas, you are intolerable."

"There's also a secret that you should ask my brother about, Mr. Detective," said Silas Reeve as he lurched past his niece and toward the door. "It has to do with the play that made him so famous and fabulously rich."

As the young woman escorted us to her father's room, she said, "I must apologize for my uncle. He's never gotten over my father's success and the riches it brought, even though Uncle Silas has benefited from them all his life. I suppose that often occurs when the younger brother eclipses the older. It's a theme that I urged my father to turn into a play, but he loves Silas too much to exploit their relationship. Daddy is a good man, Mr. Holmes, but now he's old, ill, and obviously troubled, so please be gentle and don't tire him with your questions."

My first impression upon seeing Martin Reeve lying in his bed was that Holmes and I had wasted our time. The small, thin, and pale figure I saw was clearly suffering from heart failure that in my cursory observation would claim his life within a year, if not sooner. A person of such advanced age and physical decline was also susceptible to increasing mental deterioration. Yet, as Holmes approached the bed, Reeve became quite animated. Lifting his head with great effort, he said to Dr. Manners, "Harvey, I wish to speak to Mr. Holmes and Dr. Watson alone."

"Of course, Martin. If you need me, I'll be downstairs."

When the doctor withdrew, Reeve sat up and declared, "With all this whispering, I've been hearing that I'm not long for this world," he said as he sat up, "you'd think a great man was dying. Well, I'm not great, Mr. Holmes. But the man who wrote *The Road is Narrow* was."

"Indeed so, sir. It's a classic of the theater. You are justified in being proud of it."

"You don't understand," said the old man impatiently, "I am not the man who wrote it."

While this statement resulted in Holmes exhibiting a rare expression of astonishment, I attributed the sensational remark to mental decline.

"The true author died thirty-five years ago," Reeve continued, "but I saw him two nights ago in this very room. He was a young friend of mine, Colin McGrath. There was no mistaking his blue eyes and long golden hair."

Still suspecting dementia, I asked, "Why did you put your name on the play?"

"I started as a lawyer's clerk in Chiswick. Colin lived in the same town, and we became great friends. One day, he gave me the manuscript of his play. I realized that it was the work of a genius. A few weeks later, he committed suicide without telling anyone about the play but me. To my shame, I put my name on it. Now that I'm dying, I need to make amends. That was why I did not object when Dr. Manners informed me you would be visiting me. He thinks somebody is trying to kill me. Utter nonsense. Now that you're here I want you to find out if Colin McGrath has any heirs. He married a local girl whose name I've forgotten, and I heard later that she'd had a child. Assuming she did and that the girl or boy survived into adulthood, or may have become a parent and possibly a grandparent by now, I intend to change my will to leave whoever may be in some way related to Colin half of my estate. I need to know if there is such a person or more than one. Will you find out for me, Mr. Holmes?"

"Have you told anyone else this remarkable story?"

"Knowing that I'm dying, I had to tell someone. I confided in my daughter and brother, Dr. Manners and my secretary."

"Have you informed them of your intention to alter your will?"

"I only finally decided today. Now, gentlemen, I'm feeling tired and need to sleep. Mr. Holmes, please don't deny this old fraud his dying wish."

Leaving him to rest, Holmes paused outside the bedroom door and whispered, "I am convinced that what Mr. Reeve saw was no apparition and that he is in mortal danger. For that reason, I need to remain close to this house. I've asked Kingslake to arrange a room at the inn in Carlisle. As to Mr. Reeve's desire to learn about any possible descendants, I'm entrusting that investigation to you. The place to begin is Chiswick. It's a very small town, and I'm certain that the name of a young man who left a wife and child and committed suicide is by now part of the local lore. I suggest you begin by looking up the village postmaster."

That person turned out to be a very large, elderly, and fortunately gossipy woman who had succeeded to the position upon the death of her husband. My mention of the name Colin McGrath elicited a shaking of her head, a look of disgust and the exclamation, "That cad! It was good riddance to him. I remember the scandal as if it happened yesterday. He married poor old Mrs. Northrip's granddaughter Susan, and when he found out she was expecting a baby, he up and skipped out. Not long after, we heard that he hanged himself. I wish I could say I felt sorry, but I didn't. Not for a minute."

"Do you know what happened to the wife and child?"

"She died soon after having the boy. What became of him I have no idea. I know that he was put in an orphanage. The person you should be talking to about that is the vicar. He may be High Church, but he don't let that stand in the way of helping out those who aren't, as in the matter of assisting that poor young widow in burying her good for nothing, runaway husband and then arranging for the boy to be placed in a private orphanage, instead of letting him wind up in a workhouse for parentless boys."

Short, stout and almost entirely bald, the Reverend Mr. Norman Miller reminded me of every clergyman I had encountered in the course of Holmes's investigations, in that he was so pompous and judgmental that I wondered if aspirants to the ecclesiastical collar received training in those traits while at seminary. Informed of my interest in Colin McGrath, he formed long fingers into a steeple beneath a pointed chin, clucked his tongue, and said, "While Colin was always a highly strung youth with flashes of genius, I never expected him to be capable of taking his own life. Naturally, he could not be interred in sacred ground, and because there was no money, I had to make other arrangements. After Susan died, of a broken heart I believe, I also had the sad duty to see that their child was placed in an orphanage in Liverpool. I vividly remember the lad crying his heart out. He had his mother's radiant blue eyes, but did not inherit his father's golden tresses. He would be in his late twenties now. May I ask the reason for your interest in this long-ago family tragedy?"

"That child, if he's still alive," I said, "stands to inherit half a fortune."

"Good gracious! If it will help, I have a photograph of the boy with his mother at the time of the boy's baptism."

"You must also have a record of the boy's given name."

"Alas, we had a fire years and years ago. The only reason I have the photograph is that it was in the rectory in a private picture archive I keep of children I baptized."

"May I borrow the picture? It will be returned promptly."

"If it means good fortune at last for the lad, it must be God's will that you take it. You may have difficulty in finding the young man. It is the policy of the orphanage not to reveal the names of adoptive parents."

Excited by the results of my investigation, I reported to Holmes at the inn and waited as he studied the photograph. After a few moments, he said, "Your efforts at investigation have solved one part of this mystery, Watson."

"Really? I don't see how. That photograph is decades old."

"Surely, you've noticed the resemblance of Hugh Kingslake to this young woman!"

"Good heavens, are you saying that Kingslake is Colin McGrath's son?"

"You said that the vicar remarked upon the boy having his mother's blue eyes. Nature is as unpredictable as photography is reliable. If I were to show you a picture of my mother, you would recognize my brother Mycroft, whereas I strongly resemble our father. I venture to predict that one day science will devise a means of tracing familial relationships by a comparison of blood samples. I am convinced that blood carries the blueprint of the person. In Hugh Kingslake, this produced his mother's blue eyes, but not his father's hair color. This was easily remedied by Kingslake's use of a blond wig."

"Why should Kingslake wish to kill Martin Reeve?"

"Revenge comes to mind."

"If you suppose that the revenge was motivated by Reeve's theft of Colin McGrath's play, your conjecture rests on Kingslake knowing of that episode, yet these apparitions began before Reeve told anyone that he'd stolen the play. There is also no proof that Hugh Kingslake is the son of Colin McGrath. The blue eyes may be coincidence."

"Is it also coincidence that Kingslake is in his twenties? Kingslake told us he lost his parents as a child. Coincidence? Is it by chance that he is Martin Reeve's secretary?"

"If Kingslake wished to kill Reeve, why go through all this dressing up as his father's ghost? Why not just murder him by administering poison or suffocating him with a pillow?"

"Kingslake is too clever for that, when with a bit of play-acting he could bring on death by provoking a heart attack in a man everyone knows suffers from hereditary heart disease."

"But why do all this now? Kingslake has been working for Reeve for three years."

"Watson, you have again shown that while you are not luminous, you are a conductor of light. You raise the very point that has eluded me. What has occurred recently that might have been the spark that set Kingslake off?"

"The revival of *The Road is Narrow*!"

"And what else?"

"I'm sorry, but nothing occurs to me."

"Martin Reeve told his daughter, brother, and Kingslake that he is not the play's author. Now there has been another event that Kingslake could not have anticipated."

"I'm sorry, you've lost me."

"Sherlock Holmes has arrived on the scene to investigate,

and thanks to his able associate and good friend Dr. John H. Watson the mystery is about to be dispelled. It's much too late to do so now. We'll call on Mr. Reeve first thing in the morning."

"Proceed carefully, Holmes. When the old man is told that Hugh Kingslake is the son of Colin McGrath, it will come as quite a shock. If you follow that information with your belief that Hugh Kingslake has been trying to murder him, the result could be a fatal attack."

"Quite right, Watson, but there will be a physician present when I inform him."

"Ah, yes. You refer to Dr. Manners."

"No, Watson," said Holmes with a laugh as he dipped a hand into his coat pocket and drew out a favorite old and battered briar pipe that he always took with him when we were away from Baker Street. "I mean you!"

Just past ten o'clock, as we entered a carriage that had been arranged for us by the inn keeper, a misty rain and brooding slate-gray clouds created a gloomy atmosphere that seemed appropriate to our task. After telling Martin Reeve that we had located the son of the man Reeve felt he had betrayed, we would have to inform him that the very person he had asked us to find had been attempting to frighten him to death by posing as Colin McGrath's ghost.

While I was pondering this scenario, Holmes suddenly stirred from his silence and said, "This situation is right out of Shakespeare."

"There are moments, Holmes, when I believe you are a mind reader."

"As in *Hamlet*, we have a spirit," he continued, "but in this instance it is the son of the wronged dead man playing the role of the apparition. In the words of that old Scottish prayer,

'From ghoulies and ghosties and long-leggety beasties, and things that go bump in the night, Good Lord, deliver us.' "

Presently, as our carriage drew up in pouring rain in front of Martin Reeve's imposing house, Dr. Manners rushed from within and exclaimed, "It happened again last evening, Mr. Holmes. The shock has left the old man even closer to death's door."

"Who is in the house at the moment?"

"His brother is in Martin's room keeping a bedside vigil. Catherine and Hugh Kingslake are in the parlor. The timing of Martin's turn for the worst has left them extremely distraught at a moment that should be a joyous one for them."

"Why is that?"

"This is the day they were planning to tell Martin they've become engaged to marry."

"Well, well," said Holmes, "how very interesting."

When we entered the parlor, Catherine was seated on a divan beside Kingslake with her face wet with tears. Looking up, Kingslake said, "Mr. Holmes. I'm surprised to see you. Have you heard that Mr. Reeve has suffered another attack?"

"Yes. As to surprises, this seems to be the day for them. I understand that Catherine and you have become engaged."

"She accepted my proposal last night."

"Before or after you posed as your father's ghost?"

Kingslake bolted off the divan and demanded, "What are you talking about?"

"I'm talking about a scheme by the son of Colin McGrath to frighten Martin Reeve to death, marry his daughter, and live the rest of his life on her inheritance. When did you learn that you were Colin McGrath's son?"

"This is preposterous. I am not Colin McGrath's son."

"No? I have reason to believe you are. But if you insist you are not, then Dr. Watson and I will have to continue our search so that we can inform the actual son of Colin McGrath that upon the death of Mr. Reeve, he will be able to claim half of Mr. Reeve's estate. That is why your employer is determined to alter his last will and testament."

"As Colin McGrath's son, I stand to inherit half of everything?"

"Do you now admit that your are Colin McGrath's son?"

"Yes, it's true."

"When did you realize that fact? Was it three years ago?"

"I've known it since I was a child in the orphanage. That fool of a vicar came to visit me one day and let it slip. When I demanded to know how my parents died, he told me the whole story. I was later adopted by the Kingslakes. It was only after Mr. Reeve told me that he had stolen my father's play that I decided to take revenge on him in the form of my father's ghost."

"Your scheme went beyond murder, however," said Holmes,. "You intended to make your revenge sweeter by marrying his daughter and sharing in the inheritance she received as a result of your dastardly and cruel plot!"

"You're wrong there, Mr. Holmes," Kingslake objected. Turning toward the shocked young and taking her hand, he said, "I fell in love with you the moment I saw you."

"Yet you went ahead with your devilish plan to murder her father," I contemptuously interjected. "You are a villainous cad."

From the floor above at that moment the terrified voice of Silas Reeve shouted, "Fire! Help! Martin's room is on fire!"

As we all raced for the stairs, Hugh Kingslake dashed ahead of us, pushed past Silas Reeve and plunged into the blazing bedroom.

"It was an accident," cried Silas. "I bumped a table and knocked over an oil lamp. I did my best to put out the flames, but before I knew it, the whole room was going up."

By the time the fire brigade could be summoned and they arrived, the bedroom was a blackened and smoky ruin, Martin Reeve was dead and Hugh Kingslake so seriously burned that I saw little hope for his survival.

"It's ironic," said Holmes as we gathered in the parlor, "that the man who was trying to murder Martin Reeve will probably die as the result of trying to save the life of the man he had been trying to kill. The motive for this daring action, of course, was to ensure that Mr. Reeve survived long enough to change his will, giving Colin McGrath's son half his fortune. As to the fire, I cannot prove it, but I believe Silas set it because Mr. Reeve told him that he planned to change his will to leave half of his estate to a descendant or descendants of Colin McGrath."

"Mr. Detective know-it-all," shouted Silas, "that is a bloody lie."

"However, you will probably continue to claim that the fire was the accidental act of the drunken brother overturning a lamp. My regret, you scoundrel, is that I can do nothing to bar you from your inheritance."

"Well, there'll be nothing for the man who was trying to kill my brother, either. That is, if Kingslake survives. Martin's old will is the one that applies."

A few days after Holmes and I returned to Baker Street, Dr. Manners informed us in a letter that Hugh Kingslake had died in hospital. In the months that ensued, Catherine and Silas Reeve were judged by a probate court to be Martin Reeve's sole beneficiaries.

"If I were a playwright," said Holmes, "I could write a drama based on these events that would do very well in the West End.

British audiences do seem to have a taste for the murder mystery. And justifiably so. As our friend Inspector Lestrade once said to me, 'When it comes to people killing each other by ingenious ways, nobody tops the English.' "

· 12 ·

The Darlington Substitution

*I*n the months following the fateful day on which I was introduced to Sherlock Holmes in the chemistry laboratory of St. Bartholomew's Hospital and we agreed to split the rental for a suite of rooms at 221B Baker Street, income for both of us was scarce. I was subsisting on an army pension of eleven shillings and sixpence a day and planning to establish a medical practice. Whatever came Holmes's way was from his unique profession of "private consulting detective." It was a calling that would eventually leave him wealthy. In a city even more overstocked with doctors than lawyers, medicine would ultimately afford me a comfortable living, but it was my lengthy association with Holmes and the friendship and mutual respect developed in the course of my astonishing and exiting adventures within his world that gave me rewards that cannot be measured in money and material trappings.

During those early days when I had no patients and Holmes had few clients, I found myself engaged in the fascinating pastime of observing him. Although I adjusted to idleness, he continually railed against inactivity. This impatience was exemplified one morning a month after we settled into our lodgings as he suddenly exclaimed, "What is the use of having brains if there are no crimes and no criminals? I know well that I have it in me to make my name famous, yet here I sit with nothing to challenge me and two months in arrears in my share of the rent. I'm afraid you struck a poor bargain when you came in with me, Watson."

"Not at all," said I as I left my chair and stood at a window in the hope of relieving the cramp that had seized my wounded leg. "Things are bound to pick up."

"Your optimism is surpassed only by your patient nature."

For nearly an hour, he had been carefully examining the personal notices in the daily newspapers that he referred to as agony columns. Flinging them aside, he complained, "What a rag bag of bizarre happenings and a chorus of groans, cries, and wails. There is the woman who advertised seeking the man who found her lost black boa and turned it in to the commissionaire at the Princess Skating Club. Or what about the lady who fainted on the top deck of the Brixton bus and wishes to meet the gentleman who came to her aid? Twaddle! The news pages are even less rewarding. It's as though the entire criminal class has gone on vacation and taken anyone who might benefit from my assistance with them."

"Not everyone, I think. There is a fellow across the street who has been looking at the house numbers and is now standing opposite and gazing this way. He appears to be working up the nerve to cross the street and ring our bell. Come and see."

After studying the pacing figure, Holmes ventured, "Something troubles him a great deal. That he has smoked five cigarettes and ground out the stubs on the pavement indicate that he is both anxious and angry. What do you make of him?"

"His flashy clothes and the pointy waxed mustache suggest a foreigner."

"Never judge a book by its cover, Watson, and always assess a man by the manner in which he moves. Light agility invariably suggest Latins, a heavy tread a German, and the brash stride can only be that of an American. This fellow has the controlled gait of an Englishman, but he spends considerable time in Paris. The wardrobe and waxed mustache are in the current style of Champs Elysee fashion plates. Ah! He's made up his mind, Watson. Mrs. Hudson will be bringing him up in a few moments."

I had frequently pondered what our landlady thought of the people of different classes of society who came to visit Holmes. They appeared at all hours of the day and sometimes late at night, many in a state of extreme agitation. Like me, Mrs. Hudson soon became accustomed to the arrival of Inspector Lestrade or other representative of the police who grudgingly resorted to Holmes to sort out a baffling case. On several occasions in those early days, I was amazed that he was able to listen to an account of the facts and provide the solution without stirring from his chair. Even more astonishing was the first occasion when he turned to me and declared, "Come along, Watson. You and I have urgent business in which you will be of invaluable assistance."

The gentleman Mrs. Hudson escorted to our first-floor suite in this instance introduced himself as Reginald Tremayne. His demeanor proved as brusque as his garments were fashionable and his black mustache heavily waxed. Declining my invitation to take a chair, he declared, "I have come to you, Holmes, because I need protection. My life has been threatened. The police would do nothing for me. A sallow-faced official named Lestrade, gave me your address."

"Who has threatened you?"

"My cousin."

"I'm not interested in becoming involved in family squabbles."

"Really? I was under the impression that private detectives will do anything for money. I am prepared to pay you twenty pounds to call upon Lord Darlington and warn him to desist in these threats to thrash me within an inch of my life."

"My word," I exclaimed, "Lord Darlington is the cousin in question?"

"You seem to be as readily impressed with an aristocratic title as that person Lestrade. When I mentioned Lord Darlington, he immediately brushed me off and recommended I see you. I note an array of pipes on your mantle, so I'm sure you will not object to my smoking?"

"Not in the least."

Tremayne opened a gold cigarette case that was half empty and held it out to Holmes. "Would you care to join me?"

"Thank you, I would."

Proffering the case to me, he asked, "And you, sir?"

"Cigarettes have never appealed to me. I prefer a pipe or cigar,"

"These are a blend of Turkish Latakia and Virginia cavendish made especially for me by a wonderful tobacconist in Rue Lepic."

"Before I would even consider taking you as a client," said Holmes as they both lit the cigarettes, "I need to know why your cousin has threatened you."

Tremayne exhaled a plume of smoke. "That is quite impossible."

"In that case," I interjected, "good day to you, sir."

"And who, may I ask," retorted Tremayne, "are you?"

"This is my associate," said Holmes. "Very well, I shall convey your sentiment to Lord Darlington this afternoon. The twenty pounds are payable in advance."

"When Parliament is sitting, he opens his London house. You will find him there. I know because I called on him not more than an hour ago."

With the money handed over in four crisp five-pound notes and Tremayne departed, I gazed at Holmes and demanded, "How could you agree to do business with such an insufferable creature? It would be twenty pounds well-spent to see Lord Darlington thrash him."

"It's not the twenty pounds in compensation, Watson, as welcome as the money is. It's the intriguing question of why Lord Darlington has gone to the extreme of issuing a threat of violence when he could refer the matter to the courts. I detect the odor of the fear of scandal."

"Involving Lord Darlington? Impossible. He has always been a man with an impeccable reputation. Distinguished member of the House of Lords! Upstanding family man."

"All excellent reasons to avoid a scandal. Get your hat, old man. We're off to see Lord Darlington and earn his cousin's twenty pounds."

Greeted at the door of Lord Darlington's home by an elderly butler, we were informed that we were expected and told to wait in the drawing room.

"We are expected?" I said to Holmes. "How could Lord Darlington be expecting us?"

"Obviously, he was alerted to that possibility by Lestrade.

The inspector may be slow on the uptake in the area of criminal investigation, but he's quick to act when nobility is involved."

A short, stout middle-aged gentleman with a mane of silver hair and ruddy complexion of a person familiar with fine spirits, Lord Darlington proved to be a man accustomed to getting to the point. "I have no idea how much my bounder of a cousin is paying you, Mr. Holmes, to take part in his extortionate scheme," he began, "but I will give you a thousand pounds to forget all about this matter."

"So it is blackmail," Holmes replied.

"It's bluster and arrogance," said Lord Darlington as he poured himself a large tumbler of whiskey. "Will you gentlemen join me in a bracing libation?"

"Thank you, but no," said Holmes. "I observe that when Reginald Tremayne was here this morning, you and he had words on this matter."

"He told you about it?"

"He informed me that he had called on you today. The evidence of your spirited conversation is found in the ashtray on the table. Your cousin smoked three of his special cigarettes and ground them out with considerable force. Only an angry man does that."

"Reginald has always been a scoundrel and opportunist. He is an expatriate because his name is synonymous with trouble. He lives high in Paris and is so hard up that he'll do anything to get the money required to maintain his dissolute life."

"How much is he demanding?"

After a sip of whiskey, Lord Darlington said, "Inspector Lestrade assures me that you are a man of utmost discretion, Mr. Holmes, so I will tell you everything, trusting that what I tell you will be kept in strictest confidence."

"The fee paid by your cousin is for the purpose of warning you not to thrash him, as he so inelegantly put it. Consider yourself warned. Having disposed of that obligation, I am at your service, as is Dr. Watson."

"A few days ago," said Lord Darlington as he bade us to sit, "Reginald returned from a few days of carousing in the pubs and flesh pots of Brighton with the fantastic allegation that my infant son is not in fact mine, but the child of a woman named Maude Harris. She was the hired companion of my wife when Clara traveled to a private hospital in Surrey to give birth under the care of Dr. Edwin Godfrey. Harris was also expecting. This was a year ago. I was in Geneva at the time on business. Reginald came to me with a scurrilous story that Clara had a stillborn son and that after Maude Harris also gave birth to a boy, she was paid to give the child to Clara to pass off as her own. Now Reginald is threatening to take the story to the newspapers if I don't give him ten thousand pounds. He met Maude Harris at Brighton, and they came up with this outrageous extortion plot. He says if I don't pay, she will present a sworn statement to the press."

"The problem is easily resolved," said Holmes. "Dr. Watson and I will go down to Surrey and see Dr. Godfrey. If the boy was born to your wife, that's the end of the matter. If not, you'll have to either make the issue public or submit to your cousin's demands. If Maude Harris's story is true, I recommend the former. Pay a blackmailer once, and you pay all your life."

"Go to Surrey, Mr. Holmes. See Dr. Godfrey. I must know the truth."

In the first of many of such sojourns from London in which I would find myself invited to accompany Holmes on behalf of clients, in response to an appeal from the police for assistance, or just to satisfy his own curiosity concerning a problem, he gave what amounted to a lecture on the subject of blackmail. "It is the most difficult kind of crime to resolve," he concluded, "because it is founded on the victim's fear of public exposure of indiscreet behavior by people who ought to have known better. Women are the easiest prey. It's unusual to encounter an instance in which the blackmailer is a blood relative."

"I knew Reginald Tremayne was no good the moment I laid eyes on him. He's in for a rude awakening when he learns that you are acting on behalf of Lord Darlington. The bounder will rue the day that he took Lestrade's advice and came to you."

"You assume that Maude Harris's story about the substitution of her child for the boy that Mrs. Darlington lost is false. We may discover that it isn't. You must also prepare yourself for the possibility of Dr. Godfrey's being an accomplice in this sordid business."

With the unpleasant idea planted in my mind that a member of my profession would be involved in such perfidy, I began to appreciate the complexity of Holmes's mind and why he had devoted himself to pursuing an unusual career in which nothing could be accepted on its face. It was my first inkling that Sherlock Holmes possessed not only a suspicious mind, but a deep well of cynicism.

Informed by the railway stationmaster that Dr. Godfrey resided in a small cottage with a thatched roof at the end of a country lane, we found the address within easy walking distance. It was verified by a shingle bearing his name on the front door. Three bottles of milk and the morning newspaper lay upon the stoop, and no lights were on in the windows as Holmes rang the bell. When it went unanswered, I said, "Evidently no one is at home. Dr. Godfrey may have been called away to attend to a patient. Perhaps we should have advised him by telegram to expect us."

"Something is amiss, Watson. If Godfrey were called away, why is today's delivery of milk and the daily newspaper on the doorstep? It's also curious that a village doctor who's gone out on a call would not post a note to that effect for the benefit of patients who might drop by." After again ringing the bell with no response, he tried the latch. When the door swung open, he said, "This is rather curious! What doctor do you know, Watson, who goes out and leaves his door unlocked?"

Convinced that something indeed was amiss, I asked, "Do you think we should go in?"

"This is no time to stand on ceremony."

Entering a small vestibule, Holmes picked up a lamp, lit it and called, "Anyone at home? Dr. Godfrey? Are you there?"

A moment later, we entered Dr. Godfrey's office and found him slumped over his desk with a dagger protruding from the middle of his back. He had been dead for at least a day.

"We had better notify the local constable," said I.

"In due course, Watson. Once I've had a look around this room."

"What do you expect to find?"

"I'll know it when I see it."

For the next few minutes, he was alternately on knees on the floor and examining items on and around the dead man's desk. Fascinated and amused by his resemblance to a sniffing hound, I remained silent while he studied the handle of the knife, the carpeting, a large ashtray on a table adjacent to a chair in front of the desk, and a single whiskey glass on a sideboard.

"We can bring in the police now, Watson. The murderer has made the fatal mistake of identifying himself. If you have a look at the rim of the whiskey glass, you will see particles of mustache wax. Examine the ashtray and you'll find the stubs of three cigarettes made from a blend of Latakia and Virginia cavendish. Reginald Tremayne might as well have left a signed confession. After I apprise the police of the facts, I shall ask them to delay the issuing of an arrest warrant until they hear from me. Meanwhile, you and I will return to London and resolve the matter of the Darlington substitution."

Understandably reticent to delay action, the local chief constable was persuaded to do so when Holmes threatened to refuse to provide his evidence, without which there would be no way of obtaining Tremayne's conviction. As we left the police station, I could not resist pointing out to Holmes that he had in effect blackmailed the police into acceding to his plan.

"You are quite right, Watson," he replied with a laugh. "England is fortunate that I did not decide to become a criminal."

Although there would be many occasions when Holmes would choose not to inform me of the details of his course of action, his means of bringing Reginald Tremayne to justice and of proving the parentage of the child in question required my assistance in a trick. It took the form of a plumber's tool. Much like a large firecracker in appearance, it was a smoke bomb that revealed leaks when inserted into a gas or water pipe.

"When Tremayne and Harris meet with Lord Darlington," Holmes explained, "I shall at some point tug on my left ear lobe. That is your cue."

"How can you be certain they will accept your invitation to this meeting?"

"It won't come from me. Lord Darlington will send

Tremayne a telegram that I compose in which he agrees to pay the ten thousand pounds on the conditions that both Tremayne and his accomplice are there, that the payment is made with Lady Darlington, and the child present, and that you and I are in attendance as witnesses. I shall also inform Tremayne by telegram that it is I who made these arrangements in my capacity as his agent. A third message will go to Lestrade advising him that if he follows my instructions, he will add to his record of successes by taking a murderer into custody on behalf of the Surrey police."

Exhibiting the intricate planning of a first-rate theatrical impresario, Holmes assembled the cast of characters for a drama whose climax and ending only he knew. The setting was Lord Darlington's parlor. As Holmes's unwitting foil, Reginald Tremayne made an entrance worthy of a flamboyant central figure in an Oscar Wilde play, bowing slightly in greeting Lady Darlington. Maude Harris stepped onto the stage as though she were making her sage debut in a role that she believed would make her wealthy.

"I'm glad that you've decided to do the wise thing, cousin dear," said Tremayne with a gloating grin, "and spared your charming wife and child from a terrible scandal."

"You have Mr. Holmes to thank," said Lord Darlington. "He persuaded me that I had no choice but to accede to your demands."

"As a token of my gratitude, Mr. Holmes," said Tremayne, "I shall treble your fee. Now may we get down to business?"

With that, Lord Darlington took ten thousand pounds from his desk and counted it out. As the last one-hundred pound note was stuffed by Maude Harris into her purse Holmes tugged his ear. Standing in a corner of the room where I could not be observed, I drew the plumber's rocket from my pocket, ignited it, cast it aside and shouted, "Fire!"

Through the smoke, I watched Maude Harris clutching her purse and turning toward the door. Lady Darlington swept the terrified young boy into her arms. At that moment, Holmes took a police whistle from his vest pocket and blew it loudly, resulting in Lestrade and two policemen barging into the room.

"You may arrest Reginald Tremayne on the charge of murdering Dr. Godfrey of Surrey," exclaimed Holmes, "and both him and his accomplice, Maude Harris, for the crime of blackmail. I shall provide the proof of all these charges. The evidence of extortion is the ten thousand pounds in Harris's purse. The notes were marked by Lord Darlington with his initials."

Holmes's reward from his lordship for his resolution of the case was a cheque for the very amount that Reginald Tremayne had hoped would finance life in Paris with Maude Harris. On the afternoon that a messenger from the House of Lords delivered the payment, Holmes held up the cheque as if it were a flag of victory and exclaimed, "Tonight we dine at Simpson's."

"Your means of discovering which of them gave birth to the boy was ingenious."

"I would like to claim credit for brilliance, Watson, but it belongs to King Solomon. You will recall from your childhood Bible studies, I'm sure, that he was faced with a similar case of identity. I could not propose, as he did, to cut the disputed child in half, hence my resort to a smoke bomb and your alarm of fire. The true mother grabbed the child."

Six years later, Holmes returned to the use of a plumber's rocket and my shouting about a fire to trick Irene Adler into revealing the hiding place of a photograph that might have resulted in a scandal in Bohemia. By then, Holmes had become renowned for his abilities in detection, and Mrs. Hudson never had to worry about him being late in remitting the rent.

· 13 ·

The Adventure
of Maltree Abbey

The greatest mystery to perplex me in the more than two decades of my association with Sherlock Holmes was that he was not accorded the honor of public recognition for his services in the form of a title conferred by the monarchy. This does not mean that he coveted it. After the affair of the Bruce-Partington plans, he actually declined to allow his name to go on the list. He felt that the matter was too sensitive to be called to the public's attention. However, I knew that he occasionally chafed at the lack of recognition. He told me that he could not agree with those who ranked modesty among the virtues. He was proud of his contributions to the security and the welfare of the citizens of London, and to Crown and country, and he was keenly conscious of social standing, if not always respectful of it. Each year, when Buckingham Palace published its honors list, he made note of who had been awarded a knighthood, and what titles had been conferred, and why. On one occasion when a name on the list struck him as undeserving, he dismissed the event by stating that it proved his theory that what one did in the world was not as important as making people believe what one had done was worthy of accolades.

My notes and published accounts of cases came to include an astonishing roster of the high and mighty and titles of every order, from the king of Bohemia to dukes, marquises, earls, viscounts, barons, lords, and ladies, counts and countesses, those with courtesy titles, and political figures with and without royal awards. His familiarity with the nobility and aristocracy of Great Britain was such that he rarely had to refer to *Burke's Peerage*. Interest in the roots of the English gentry and of venerable families in general resulted in his studying and then publishing a history of early English charters. I was not therefore surprised that Holmes accepted a case presented to us on a December afternoon by the sister of the fourteenth earl of Maltree. Dressed in high Edwardian fashion with a fur boa and a broad-brimmed hat, Sybil Carter was as attractive and vivacious as she was direct in stating the purpose of her visit, although directness is not the same thing as clarity.

"I can tell you my problem in two words: Jonathan Devers," she declared. "Although he has become a millionaire because of his acumen in the world of investment and finance, he is an awful man. He wanted to marry me, but even to save the Maltree estate from receivership, that was quite out of the question. Well, Jonathan suggested that my brother Harold, the poorest of all the earls of Maltree, leave the country and disappear.

Harold is dead set against any outside interference, so I thought that because we play the music tomorrow night, and knowing that you play the violin, Mr. Holmes, I was hoping that you could be there."

"Excuse me, Miss Carter," said Holmes, "but I find it difficult to follow you."

"Oh? I thought I covered everything."

"I gather that the crux of your situation is that you and your brother find yourselves in severe financial difficulty. Am I correct?"

"We're in a dreadful way, due to a loss last year after Harold invested nearly all we had in Canadian copper. The market dropped, you see, and now we're nearly wiped out, and Maltree Abbey totters on the brink of bankruptcy. That's where Jonathan Devers comes in. He's a cousin from South Africa and extremely rich, but he is such a bore that I couldn't marry him, even for the sake of Maltree Abbey. Jonathan offered Harold fifty thousand pounds if Harold would go abroad and pretend to disappear."

"What would be the effect," I asked, "of that ridiculous scheme?"

Holmes answered, "If the heir were to die or to vanish, the estate would pass to her and into the hands of Jonathan Devers by reason of wedlock, and since he is a cousin the Crown might very well grant him the title of earl."

"Exactly right, Mr. Holmes."

"This is a really a family matter, Miss Carter. Because there has been no crime, I cannot help you. I'm very sorry. You need a solicitor, not a detective."

"But you can! Please hear me out, sir."

"Very well. Pray continue."

"I hoped that you could persuade Jonathan to go away. This

is why I want you to come to the abbey tomorrow under the guise of being interested in the music ritual. When the first earl of Maltree was created by Henry the Eighth, after he abolished all the monasteries, Henry gave the family a motto. In Latin inscribed in our private chapel at Maltree Abbey, it states, 'If the Maltrees be in need, seek the Venerable Bede.' "

"Excuse me," said I as I took notes. "Venerable what?"

"*Bede*," she responded. "Spelled B-e-d-e."

"Correct me if I'm wrong, Miss Carter," said Holmes. "Your Bede was an eighth-century monk who was revered not only as a holy man, but as the first great historian of England."

"Yes. We have a statue of him in our chapel. We also have a family custom related to it that involves music. It's been passed down in the family that if ever the family is in trouble, we should play a particular tune that was composed by King Henry himself."

"Your ritual isn't unique," said I. "You might be surprised to know that many of the old families of England have superstitions. For example, the Musgraves of Hurlstone inherited a ritual in the form of riddle that seemed to have all the aspects of a child's treasure hunt. It was in fact a set of directions to a buried historic treasure. And there was the fascinating document of the Baskervilles that—"

"Yes, Watson," Holmes exclaimed irritably, "but I'm sure my previous cases are of no interest to this lady."

"My brother knows nothing about my coming to see you, so I thought that you could say that you came to hear the music, what with your being interested in music as a violin player. If you take the first morning express from King's Cross to Chipping Martin in Yorkshire, Yorkshire is closer to where Bede lived, although any northern county would probably be all right. I believe King's Cross would be the right station for trains to the north, but you might want to check this. You'll be at Maltree Abbey in plenty of time. Don't worry about your fee. We're not completely broke."

As I escorted the young woman down the stairs and hailed a hansom cab to take her to King's Cross Station, I ruminated upon the fact that Sybil Carter of Maltree Abbey had added her name to a long roster of women who had either sought Holmes's assistance or otherwise benefited from his activities. They ran the social and economic gamut from a Bloomsbury landlady who was concerned about a new lodger with elusive habits, the betrayed wife of a Russian nihilist, Elsie Cubitt in the case involving a code that resembled dancing men, a California heiress who disappeared from her wedding celebrations, and the *danseuse* Flora Millar to Lady Brackenstall, Lady Frances Carfax, and Violet de Merville, daughter of the general of Khyber fame. My notes contained numerous entries of names of governesses, maids, and other domestics who in one way or another figured in Holmes's cases. Returning from seeing Miss Carter off and finding that Holmes was donning his overcoat, I asked, "Where are you going? It's nearly dinnertime."

"To see Inspector Athelney Jones at Scotland Yard. I need to know if Jonathan Devers is known to the Metropolitan Police."

"How could he be? He's a millionaire financier who lives in South Africa."

"If Devers is so rich, why is he so determined to get his hands on Maltree Abbey? As to that piece of real estate, you can be of assistance by spending your time before dinner by looking it up in my dusty copy of Sir William Fielding's *Encyclopedia of Abolished Monasteries in the Reign of Henry VIII,* which I found very useful in my research on the topic of ancient charters."

Expecting to find the material on events that occurred in the sixteenth century dull and boring, I found myself drawn by the author's lively prose into a fascinating tale of royal scheming and dubious maneuvers by a vengeful monarch. Maltree Abbey was one of the largest ecclesiastical properties in the realm. Sprawling over thousands of acres, it consisted not only of the abbey, but ruins of a Roman fortress, vast woodlands, farmland, and a lake that was so deep that it was called "the bottomless tarn." The material also contained a brief history of the Venerable Bede and the legend of Henry VIII's providing the curious inscription cited by Miss Carter and the musical ritual she mentioned—all of which, I told Holmes when he returned, struck me as utter nonsense.

"It may well be," said Holmes, "but I recall your expressing the same opinion in the case of the Musgrave Ritual. We may find that the Maltree Abbey legend is baseless. If so, we can chalk it up as one of those whimsical facets of our country's history that set England apart and provide the government treasury more money from tourists than ever filled the coffers of Henry VIII and all the kings and queens who succeeded him. There is talk from time to time that we should abolish the monarchy. If that day ever comes, Watson, and no one comes here to see the Beefeaters of the Tower of London, ogle the Crown Jewels, and witness the changing of the guard at Buckingham Palace, England will be the loser!"

In the centuries since Henry VIII's time, the Maltree Abbey estate had dwindled in size as financially strapped ancestors of its present occupants sold off portions of the land. The abbey itself had suffered from neglect, but the stately main building with its looming bell tower was still an impressive sight. Greeting us in the great hall, the earl was a handsome young

man with such a striking resemblance to his sister that they
might have been twins. "You are very welcome, of course, he
said, "but I wish that Sybil hadn't bothered you with such a trifling matter. She's a darling, but she is overly emotional. I'll
find some way to save Maltree Abbey from bankruptcy. I've
been giving some thought to raising money by opening it to the
public, as scandalous as that might seem to some people. Would
you like to see the chapel? It's the oldest part of the estate and
by far the most interesting historically."

One of the most beautiful private chapels I had ever entered,
the example of medieval religious architecture was rendered
even more interesting by the carved wooden figure of the Venerable Bede. As if he were practicing to be a tour guide, the earl
said, "Note the delicate workmanship in the beads of the rosary
that the Bede holds. Superb, isn't it?"

Studying the artifact as closely and intently if he were
investigating the scene of a crime, Holmes said, "Fascinating,
indeed."

"Maltree Abbey," continued the earl, "was founded by monks
from Jarrow, where Bede spent most of his life, and when they
came here, they brought his relics with them."

Almost as impressive as the chapel was the dining room of
the main house. According to the history of the estate that I'd
read, the residence had been built a century after the chapel,
but with the exception of the installation of gas lighting the
large room was exactly as it was first built. When Holmes and
I joined the earl and his charming sister for dinner, Harold
Carter introduced us to their cousin. Despite Holmes's frequently voiced warning against permitting emotions to color
one's first impression of a person, I was perhaps biased because
of Miss Carter's dislike for Mr. Jonathan Devers. This feeling

of animus was reinforced when he came to table in casual attire and muddy riding boots. He then exhibited a demeanor that was downright rude.

"Sybil told me there would be distinguished company at tonight's musical soiree," said he in a condescending tone. "I supposed, however, that the guests would be more respectable."

"Really, Jonathan," objected Miss Carter. "Mr. Holmes and Dr. Watson are received in the best homes in England. Mr. Holmes is also an accomplished violinist with an interest in the music of the sixteenth century. Apologize at once or leave the table."

"Do forgive me, gentlemen," replied Devers with a grudging smile. "Coming from one of the colonies, I am not familiar with who is esteemed in England and who is not, nor with who is an expert on the niceties of old music. I happen to have a tin ear, but Sybil insists that because I am a cousin, I must attend her rendering on the piano of Bede's ancient tune."

Although I did not possess Sherlock Holmes's appreciation of music, I felt I was justified in describing what we heard in the music room after dinner as a jumble of meaningless notes. I was, therefore, displeased at having to hear them repeated again and again later on Holmes's violin in our room. After each rendering, he laid aside the instrument to light a pipe and go over the tune vocally. This went on well past midnight. As I was dozing off, Holmes shook me hard and exclaimed, "I've got it, Watson! I know the secret of Maltree Abbey."

"Are you aware of the time? Can't it wait till morning?"

"You'll have plenty of time for sleeping, Watson. Come along to Harold Carter's room and then to the chapel."

A few minutes later, we stood before the statue of Bede in the glow of candlelight. The fourteenth earl of Maltree appeared as sleepy and mystified as I when Holmes said, "Look very carefully at the figure, with special attention to the rosary."

"It's an ordinary rosary," said Carter.

"Quite so. However, history records that the rosary did not come into use until almost five centuries after the time of the Venerable Bede. Now direct your attention to the fourth bead. The number four is the key to this riddle. The fourth letter of the alphabet is d, which is also the most frequent note in the Bede's tune. I believe that the ancient song is a clever code. What is the motto of the Maltree family, Lord Carter?"

" 'If the Maltree family be in need, seek the Venerable Bede.' "

"The motto and the music are the key," said Holmes. "The note d directs us to the fourth bead in the rosary. Press it, please, Watson."

As I did so, I heard a scraping sound from behind the statue as a portion of the wooden wall opened to reveal the entrance to a passageway and a stairway leading below the chapel.

"King Henry was not only a clever monarch, but a composer of music, as his writing of *Greensleeves* attests," said Holmes as we descended in candlelight. "I have no doubt that Henry wrote the tune with the code. He also arranged to conceal in the room below something that was to be a guarantee of Maltree Abbey's solvency. As often happens over time, the meaning of the motto and the musical ritual was lost."

As we reached the bottom of the steep stairway, Carter inquired, "Are you saying that there may be a hidden treasure under the chapel?"

"If not," said Holmes, "Henry was also a cruel prankster."

With rising anticipation, I followed Holmes and Carter into a small chamber, expecting to find the kind of burial crypt that was common not only in such ancient religious edifices as St.

Paul's Cathedral and Westminster Abbey, but in chapels on family estates throughout England. I had visited many of them as a boy on excursions with my historically minded grandfather. With large sheets of paper and chunks of charcoal in hand, we'd spent hours making rubbings of the graven images in metal or stone of the occupants of the crypts. Consequently, I was surprised to find no sarcophaguses in the chamber under the Maltree Abbey chapel.

Gazing at the almost empty room in the eerie glow of our candles, I observed a crucifix on the opposite wall and beneath it a dusty table adorned by a pair of silver candlesticks, which appeared to have little intrinsic value.

"If there was ever a treasure down here," said I as Holmes examined the table, "it's long gone, probably plundered centuries ago like the tombs of Egyptian kings that were looted by grave robbers."

"There was something here, and judging by the dust. not so long ago," said Holmes. "If you look closely, gentlemen, you will see a large rectangular area of the tabletop that is free of dust. On the rest of the surface, the dust is deep, while this space has not a speck. The intruder carried a bag, probably a Gladstone. That type of satchel has metal studs on the bottom. When he set the bag down, it made four round impressions in the dust. Whatever it was that he took from this table had to be small enough to fit into the bag. What does that suggest?"

"A jewel box?" asked Carter.

"Possibly. The object was removed very recently. Look at the floor. Fresh footsteps. A man's. Riding boots, not shoes. Note the gap between the impressions of the soles and the heels. Only boots have such a gap."

"Jonathan Devers," I exclaimed. "He was wearing boots at dinner. I never trusted that man. He's the culprit. I'm sure of it."

Shaking his head, Lord Carter said, "How could Jonathan know that this room was here? He's never been to Maltree Abbey."

"Neither had I before today," I replied, "but I learned a great deal about the estate by looking it up in a book. There are libraries in South Africa. Devers could have done the same."

"Did your book reveal the existence of this secret room?"

"Well, no, but Devers could have figured out the code, just as Holmes did."

"Why should Jonathan do such a thing?"

"I suggest we find the scoundrel," I replied, "and put that very question to him."

"We can't barge in on my cousin in the middle of the night and accuse him of being a thief. I don't like him either, but we have no evidence. What say you, Mr. Holmes?"

"I find it curious that your cousin suddenly appeared at Maltree Abbey at the moment when you are in dire financial straits and then proposed that you disappear, as your sister put it, and that he marry her. I find it difficult to believe that he did all this out of familial fealty. If he is a millionaire, why not offer you a loan?"

"He probably knew I wouldn't accept one."

"These are questions that must be answered, sir, and this is no time for chivalry. Watson is right. We have no choice but to confront Devers immediately. If you haven't the stomach for it, Watson and I will do so Where is his room?"

"He's in the north wing. I'll go with you."

My hopes that Jonathan Devers was about to be exposed as a cad and a cur were dashed with the discovery that he had absconded. My only consolation was that in fleeing, he'd proved his guilt. Deeply disappointed, I said to Holmes urgently, "He's probably planning to return to South Africa. We must alert Scotland Yard at once."

"No need for that, Watson. Athelney Jones is already on the case."

To my astonishment, a few minutes later the Scotland Yard inspector appeared at the door of the Abbey with Jonathan Devers in handcuffs.

"I followed him from the house down to the lake," Jones explained. "I grabbed him as he was about to throw a Gladstone bag into the water. Naturally, I looked in the bag and I found this old book. You could have knocked me over with a feather. Why on earth, I asked myself, was he in such a hurry to heave a book into a lake?"

Taking the large, leather-bound volume from Jones, Holmes asked. "Why indeed?"

"It's my book," railed Devers. "I can do what I want with it."

"Really? Then you won't mind telling us the contents."

Devers offered no reply.

"We'll find out what it is," said Holmes. Opening the book to the title page, he held it up for all to see. The title page was in brilliant calligraphy. My schoolboy Latin was just good enough to make it out:

The Chronicle of Bede Concerning the History and Events of the Reigns of Their Majesties Edwin and Oswald from the Year 617 of Our Blessed Lord to 642.

"Good lord, it's a priceless document dating back more than a thousand years," I said in outrage, "and this monster was about to throw it into a bottomless lake!"

Inspector Jones asked, "What do I charge this man with, Mr. Holmes?"

"For now, burglary and theft will suffice to hold him until you complete your other investigation into his activities. I have no doubt that the Crown's prosecutor will have more than enough evidence of financial fraud to ensure that Jonathan Devers spends many years in prison."

A few minutes later, with Sybil and Lord Carter and myself seated in the large drawing room of Maltree Abbey and Bede's chronicle resting on a pillow on a table, Holmes said, "The explanation is complex. Devers is a millionaire, but he desires something that mere wealth can't attain. What might that be?"

I replied, "A title?"

"If he could somehow become the fifteenth earl of Maltree," Holmes continued, "he would be able to use his riches not only to restore the estate, but take his place among the aristocracy. As a financier, he was in a position to know that you, Lord Carter, had invested heavily in Canadian copper. He may have actually manipulated its disastrous decline by buying a large block of the stock and then dumping it, precipitating the crash. We won't know if that is true until the frauds division of Scotland Yard completes a secret investigation that has been going on for months. I learned of this when I called on Inspector Jones and expressed an interest in Jonathan Devers."

"So you knew from the outset," I interjected, "that Devers was a scoundrel."

"I suspected it. As you well know, Watson, I am loathe to attribute an unusual set of circumstances, such as Devers showing up at a crucial moment, to coincidence. When I heard that he had proposed a fraudulent disappearance to Lord

Carter, I had no doubt that Devers was unscrupulous and worthy of watching. Inspector Jones agreed."

"But why," said Lord Carter, "should Jonathan steal the book?"

"It's obvious," said I. "He had to make sure you didn't benefit from its discovery, as he feared might happen with Sherlock Holmes on the case."

"Your cousin is a brilliant man," said Holmes. "He managed to crack the musical code and went looking for what he thought would be a treasure, found Bede's book, and saw that it was a priceless heirloom. If you found it, that would be the end of Maltree Abbey's troubles. But it was worthless to him. He couldn't sell it, so he decided it to throw it into the lake and wait for the estate to go into bankruptcy, at which time he would buy Maltree Abbey for a pittance. As the savior of one of the country's greatest historical properties, and with plenty of money to buy influence, it would be only a matter of time until he found his name on the king's honors list."

"Thanks to Holmes and unfortunately for Devers," I ventured, "Inspector Jones caught him before he could throw the book into the lake."

"I recognized during the affair involving the Agra treasure many years ago," Holmes said, "that Athelney Jones was quite an asset to Scotland Yard. Now, as then, he proved to be quick on the uptake and welcomed the opportunity to add the name of Jonathan Devers to his growing roster of thwarted criminals. He came directly to the abbey after he and I spoke at Scotland Yard and kept his eyes on Devers's activities. When he saw the man leave the abbey in the middle of the night, carrying a bag toward the lake, he realized something sinister was afoot and thereby saved an invaluable artifact of the long and illustrious history of England."

Approximately a year later as Jonathan Devers sat in a cell in Dartmoor Prison and the owners of Maltree Abbey used the proceeds of the sale of the Venerable Bede's journal to the British Museum, the king's honors list was announced. Among those cited for their outstanding service was Athelney Jones. He was awarded Order of the British Empire.

"Once again, Holmes," I exclaimed, "you have been outrageously overlooked."

"Never mind, Watson," he said with a slight smile, "His Majesty was kind enough to send me one of those jeweled tiepins he's so fond of handing out to subjects who find his favor."

· ABOUT THE AUTHOR ·

A broadcast journalist for more than three decades, H. Paul Jeffers has published sixty works of fiction and nonfiction. A member of America's premier Sherlockian society, The Baker Street Irregulars, with the investiture name "Wilson Hargreave," he is the author of two acclaimed Sherlock Holmes patsiche novels, *The Adventure of the Stalwart Companions* and *Murder Most Irregular.* He has published a history of Scotland Yard (*Bloody Business*), two histories of the FBI, fifteen mystery novels, and several true-crime titles.

Biographies include Theodore Roosevelt; Grover Cleveland; Mayor Fiorello La Guardia; Diamond Jim Brady; Theodore Roosevelt, Jr.; Eddie Rickenbacker; and murdered 1950s movie star Sal Mineo. He has published histories of Freemasonry,

Jerusalem, the Great Depression, and the San Francisco earthquake of 1906; *The 100 Greatest Heroes*; and three lifestyle titles, *The Perfect Pipe, The Good Cigar,* and *High Spirits*.

He lives in Manhattan in an apartment that friends have described as both a museum and shrine to the Sleuth of Baker Street.